THE UNCORRUPTED CORPSE

By Greg Fowlkes

Includes previews from the book

A FICTIONAL DETECTIVE TRIFECTA

~ NOVELLAS FEATURING
THE FICTIONAL DETECTIVE ~

THE UNCORRUPTED CORPSE

© 2017 The Fictional Press
www.TheFictionalPress.com

The Fictional Press is a small, independent press specializing in the publication of fictional works by emerging authors. If you are interested in bringing your fictional works to life in print as well as electronically, contact us! We can help!

www.TheFictionalPress.com

ISBN 13: 978-1-943403-43-1

Printed in the United States of America

BOOKS BY GREG FOWLKES

From the Wizard at Law Series:
The Laws of Magic
Trial by Magic

From the Murder on Mars Series:
Blood Red Sands of Mars
A Death at Station Alpha
A Corpse in Hut Town
Murder at the Mars Club

From the Fictional Detective Series:
The Fictional Detective
A Fictional Detective Trifecta

Star City Stories: Space Opera Noir Featuring Frank Sladek

The Uncorrupted Corpse

Tequila Visions

Cargo From Paradise

Ice Viking

TABLE OF CONTENTS

EPILOGUE

They exhumed Vlad Romanescu's body today. The court order listed the reason as the need to get DNA evidence to close a couple of murder cases in Columbus, Ohio. Most of us who were involved in the case, though, just wanted to reassure ourselves that he was still there. Not that there was any rational reason to believe his body wouldn't still be in the grave, but the case had affected everyone it had touched. No matter what they *believed*, there were still doubts lingering in the dark corners of their mind.

That's why we were all there on that cold, rainy morning as they dug up the casket, Hazeltine, Murphy, the Smercheks—and myself. The Smercheks had come separately. Vern Smerchek had called me a few months earlier, just to talk I think. He hadn't been drinking. He told me that he and his wife Ellen had separated. That happens sometimes after a child dies. He said he wasn't sure if they'd get back together. I hadn't told him what I thought would happen.

Usually exhumations don't draw many people. Just the cemetery staff and the driver of the medical examiner's meat wagon, and maybe someone from the D.A.'s office if that's where the exhumation request originated. Maybe a family member or two. There was a regular crowd for this one. No family members of course. We never did find any family for Romanescu. Naturally the D.A. himself was there along with a prosecutor from Ohio. It had been a big case, thirteen bodies, not counting Romanescu. As I mentioned, Murphy was there. He had been the homicide detective working the case. Besides the Smercheks there were friends and families of some of the other victims. A couple of reporters and a crew from one of the TV station were in attendance as well.

And me. I had met many of them, but didn't say hello except to give a curt nod to Murphy. It wasn't that kind of occasion. We all just stood around grim faced as the back-hoe removed the dirt over the grave.

Finally they were done with the digging. A sling was suspended from the scoop of the back-hoe so that they could raise the casket from the hole. The workers did their thing and the coffin was lifted up and set on the grass next to the opening. It was dead quiet in that way that happens when there's a drizzle and a thick fog sets in. All you could hear was the clank of the workers' tools as they opened the casket and the sound of crows perched in the gray enshrouded trees in the distance.

They finally got the casket open. Normally they would just put the body on a gurney and hustle it away in the meat wagon as quickly as possible. The D.A. was smart though. He knew that there were people who wanted to see for themselves that the body was still there. People that needed to see. He knew, because he was one of them. So, before they moved the body, he let people file by the open box to look. They weren't gawking, they were making sure.

I took my turn after Murphy and before Hazeltine. I'd never thought Romanescu had looked all that great before he was killed. They hadn't embalmed him. Something about a clause in his will. Still, he looked about the same after six months in the ground as he had walking around. Except for the hole in the middle of his forehead where Murphy had shot him with a .38 caliber round. That and the stump of a pool cue that was still sticking out of his chest. That had been my contribution to the affair. I was glad that they hadn't removed it. Not that I believe in those kind of things. Hazeltine had strongly suggest decapitating him and placing the head in the casket face down, but the D.A. had nixed the idea as going too far. That would be an admission of something no one wanted to think about.

Everybody had their look and then the D.A. gave a nod to the M.E.'s man to take the body away. People began moving off to their cars. No one was talking. The grim expressions hadn't left their faces, either, but they looked a little more reassured now that they had seen that the body was still there.   Murphy, Hazeltine and I adjourned to a bar for the drink we all felt the need for.

ANNA SMERCHEK

1.

The couple sitting across from me looked like nice people. Hard-working, not overly prosperous, but not poor, either. They looked like they came from some small town in the middle of the state, someplace that was a decade or two behind the times and just as happy that way. I figured they were probably Lutheran and went to church most weeks.

He was around fifty, average build, slightly balding with light brown hair trimmed close. He had the look of someone that moved around a lot on the job but didn't do a lot of heavy lifting. She was maybe a few years younger and had housewife written all over her face. She was dressed neatly in a skirt and blouse with a sweater thrown over her shoulders. Neither one looked as if they had gotten much sleep lately. They didn't look the kind of people that needed a private investigator.

They had what I assumed was their daughter with them, a high-school aged girl. She was dressed much like her mother, though I thought probably not from choice. She was pretty in a small-town way and looked like she could be intelligent when it suited her. I would have guessed that she could be a bit on the wild side at times, but now she just seemed subdued.

"What can I do for you, Mr.—?" Instinctively I knew he would do most of the talking. It just struck me as that kind of relationship.

"Smerchek. Vern Smerchek. This is my wife Ellen. And my daughter Katherine."

"Mr. Smerchek, Mrs. Smerchek. Just why do you think you need a private detective?" I wasn't exactly trying to discourage the business, but people have some strange ideas, mostly from books and TV, as to what a private detective can and can't do. It was better for all parties concerned that we got things straightened out right away. It saved a lot of wasted time, especially mine.

"It's about our daughter, Anna. She's gone missing. We want you to find her."

"Missing persons is properly a police problem, Mr. Smerchek. So are run-aways."

"Anna didn't run away," Ellen Smerchek said in a surprisingly firm voice. Vern might wear the pants in the family, but I could see that his wife was a woman with her own mind. Coming to me had probably been her idea.

"We've been to the police," Vern said. "They weren't much help. They took her name and 'investigated' but they said without evidence of a crime there wasn't anything they could do."

"They are right about that, Mr. Smerchek. You'd be surprised at how many people disappear or just wander off without telling anyone. The police have limited resources. They try to use them to the best advantage. At least most of the time. Tell me, how old is your daughter, Mr. Smerchek?"

"She's nineteen."

"Above the age of consent—"

"What do you mean?"

"First off, she's her own person, independent in the eyes of the law. Second, if she saw fit to run off with some man, say to California or someplace, it's nobody's business but her own."

"Our Anna's a good girl, mister," Ellen protested. "She was raised right. She wouldn't do anything like that."

"Listen, both of you. You need to understand something. If I take this case, and that's still an open question, I might find out some things, unpleasant things, things you might not want to find out. When people go missing, particularly when young women go missing, there's usually a reason, and rarely is it a happy one. It usually involves sex, booze or drugs—-or death. Sometimes it's better just to let go."

Vern looked at Ellen. They didn't say anything. They didn't have to. I had the feeling they had had this conversation before.

"Anna didn't do drugs. She wasn't a wild girl either." Vern looked at his daughter. I could tell what he was thinking. If one of his daughters were to run off it would be Katherine.

Ellen said quietly, "Will you take the case or not?"

I thought about it for a minute. If I said no they'd just find someone else, someone without my inner nobility and high moral principles. That from a guy who peeks through keyholes to catch cheating spouses for a living. I couldn't throw the Smercheks to the wolves. They'd be easy pickings for most of the bums in my line of work.

"I'll take the case on two conditions. One is that the police have no objections. If the case is being pursued actively they won't be happy with me interfering. It could cost me my license."

"You said two conditions," Vern responded. "What's the other?"

"You can pay my fee. My usual rates are two hundred a day plus expenses."

"That's a lot of money. How do we know you'll find her?"

"You don't. The fact is she may never be found. It happens all the time. Or maybe she'll turn up twenty years from now married to a dentist in Schenectady. That happens, too, though not as often. That's why maybe you should save your money and hopes she turns up on her own."

"We can't do that," Ellen said again in her quiet firm voice. "I know something has happened to her, something bad."

"Two hundred is a lot of money," Vern said. "We aren't rich people."

I watched the two of them. I could see Vern was on the fence, but Ellen wasn't going to be dissuaded. I made a decision. I'm still not sure it was the right one.

"I'll tell you what I'll do. You look like nice people," I said sounding like a used-car salesman. "If you'll give me two-fifty, I'll look into it over the next day or two. If nothing turns up, we can drop it. If I find any leads worth following I'll tell you and you can decide whether you want to take it any further."

Vern looked at Ellen. There was that unspoken conversation again, like they had been married so long they didn't need to talk.

Vern pulled out his wallet and laid two hundred dollar bills, a pair of twenties and a ten on my desk.

I picked them up and put them in my wallet. Then I wrote him a receipt. I also handed him a contract to sign saying I was investigating on his behalf. That didn't mean anything under the law, but sometimes it gets the law to turn a blind eye.

"OK. Now that we got that out of the way, tell me a little about yourselves."

"Why do you need to know that?" Vern asked more puzzled than reluctant.

"If we are to assume that your daughter's disappearance wasn't some random act, then I need to understand her, understand her frame of mind."

"I see. I guess that makes sense." I'm not sure Vern bought it, but he had placed himself in my hands.

It turns out Vern ran a hardware store in some small town to the north that I'd heard of but never been in. The business had been in the family for three generations. Not the big time, but steady business. Ellen worked there part-time, but mostly kept the house. Both girls had worked in the store after school until Anna had gone away to college.

Anna was the first in the family to go to the university. She had had good grades in high-school, did all the usual small town things. She had been liked but had no particular boy friend. As far as the Smercheks knew she had no high-school sweetheart that might have swept her away—or kidnapped her.

She had been in her second year at the university. The first year had been fine. She got good if not spectacular grades, written home regularly, took the bus home for holidays. The pattern had repeated the second year but the calls and letters came less often until they had stopped. That was when they became concerned, but by then it was too late. She hadn't been seen in her dorm for several weeks. They had contacted the university and then the police, but she was gone.

I got the names of her professors and fellow students that she had written about in her letters. The Smercheks assured me that nothing in her letters had hinted at any problems. All this time the other daughter, Katherine, sat there staring at the corner. I couldn't quite make her out. She wasn't indifferent to her sister's disappearance, but she didn't seem to feel it like her parents. Maybe it was just sibling rivalry. I had the feeling Anna had always been the favorite.

Finally, we were done. We stood. I shook hands with Vern and Ellen. Then they left.

It was a minute or two later that the daughter, Katherine, came back into my office.

"Can I help you?" I asked curiously.

"I forgot my purse." Somehow I didn't think she had.

"Was there anything you wanted to add to what your parents told me?" I was guessing that the relationship between the two sisters had been complex. Part rivalry, part confiding. They were only a few years apart in age and Anna might well have mentioned things to her sister that she wouldn't have thought of revealing to her mother.

"I don't know if it's important—"

"Anything you know might be helpful, Katherine."

"It was something she told me when she came home for Easter last year."

Of course Anna had come home for Easter. They had probably gone to church and then had a big Sunday dinner of ham, mashed potatoes and peas along with some aunts and uncles thrown in. They had been that kind of family.

"Go on," I encouraged.

"We were talking about her courses. Anna was really excited. She always liked school. I want to go to college, myself. Not for the classes, but to just get away. I don't know if Momma will let me, now."

"Anyway, she was talking about one teacher she really liked, Professor Hazeltine. He taught a literature class. Anna was always into new things and this class was all about stories and poems and things from different cultures."

"Do you think your sister had a crush on this Professor Hazeltine?"

Katherine looked puzzled for a moment as if she were considering the possibility. "No, not that way. This Professor Hazeltine is old. But she found what he was teaching fascinating."

Myself, I wasn't so sure about the age issue. In the first place he might not be that old, and even if he were, some women are drawn to father figures. If so, it wouldn't be the first time a student-teacher relationship got more than academic.

"In what way?"

"Well, it turns out that this professor was running some sort of afterhours discussion group. Not a real class, but just a meeting with some of his students. They'd talk about all sorts of weird things like old vampire movies and magic and things like that. Anna seemed to be really interested. No one back home ever even thought of stuff like that."

I was going to ask her more about that, but there was a knock at the door. It was Vern Smerchek.

"What's taking you so long, Kate? Did you find your purse? We've got to get going. It's a long drive home."

The daughter picked up her purse and hurried out into the hallway.

"I'm sorry about that," Vern said, and then he was gone leaving me staring at the back side of the door as it closed. The younger girl had certainly given me some things to think about. I'd have to have a chat with this Hazeltine.

2.

I placed a call to the police department. As usual, they were reluctant to give out any information. It took some persuading and explaining that I was working at the family's request before I was given the name of the detective assigned to the case, Detective Sergeant James Murphy. The good news was that I knew Murphy slightly from my days on the force. The bad news was that he mostly worked homicides.

After a couple of attempts, I managed to get a hold of Murphy. He wasn't thrilled to be talking to a private investigator, even an ex-cop working for the family, but he didn't blow me off, either.

"Look, Murphy, all I really want to know is if I will be stepping on the department's toes if I start looking into the case. If so, let me know, and I'll tell the family it's still under active investigation and give them their money back."

"The case hasn't been closed yet, but between you and me it's gone about as cold as they get. The girl just vanished into thin air. I guess it won't cause problems if you stick your nose into it as long as you don't make waves."

"Thanks, Murphy. I'll try to be discrete. Should I read anything into it that they assigned it to you in particular?" We both knew what I was getting at.

"No. It was just the luck of the draw. It's hard to believe, but there was actually a shortage of murders at the time the girl was reported missing. Missing Persons was swamped though, so some of their cases were shuffled around to different departments. I ended up with the Smerchek girl."

"Any chance the other missing persons cases were related?"

"Not that anyone could discover. No patterns seemed to pop out."

I was pretty sure that Murphy was giving it to me straight. He was a good cop as far as I remembered, and not the kind of guy to play games.

"Anything else you can tell me that might save the Smerchek's some money?"

"Look, I'm kind of busy and can't really talk right now. I shouldn't really be feeding information on an active case to an outsider anyhow." He almost sounded apologetic.

"Sure, don't sweat it Murphy. I understand. And if I come across anything you should know about, I'll let you know."

I was about to hang up when Murphy asked, "Do you know the Dead End?"

The Dead End was a little bar that got its name because it was at the end of a dead end street. It wasn't much of a place, a long bar, a pool table that needed new felt and a couple of tables along the wall. It was a beer and whiskey joint. One TV that only showed sports and a juke box that mostly featured songs more than ten years old. It was only a few blocks from police headquarters and a lot of the regulars were cops, at least around shift time.

"Yeah, I know it."

"I'll be coming off shift in a few hours, We can have a beer for old time's sake."

"Sure. I'll be there. Thanks for talking to me."

I was a little surprised. Murphy knew me, but we had never been what you would call close. I figured he had something he wanted to say about the Smerchek case, something he wanted to get off his chest, something I wanted to hear.

I hadn't been in The Dead End since, well, since a slug to the knee had forced a change of careers. I got there before Murphy and sat at the bar nursing a beer. The bartender wasn't exactly cordial until one of the cops going on shift after a beer and a burger stopped to say hi. I guess then he figured I was ok. He didn't say anything, but at least he stopped looking at me every thirty seconds to check on what I was doing there.

Murphy showed up after I'd been there about fifteen minutes and sat down on the stool next to me. The bartender poured a tap and placed it in front of him without a word being exchanged.

"How's the leg?" he asked after the first sip. The leg is why I'm an ex-cop.

"It's ok. I get around alright. Just the occasional twinge when it's going to rain."

Murphy gave a grunt and took another sip of his beer. "So what's your angle on the Smerchek case?" He was talking like he had a chip on his shoulder.

"Angle? What do you mean?"

"Look, they're good people. They already have one daughter missing and their youngest is probably going to give them trouble in a year or two. They don't need some private dick taking advantage of them. How'd they end up with you, anyhow?"

"I don't know. They called me for an appointment. They probably got the number from the phone book. We met, I agreed to look into the matter for two hundred and fifty bucks. If I don't find anything worth chasing, I make a report and that's it. It was pretty clear when I talked with them that if it wasn't me, it would be someone else, someone that might milk them for all they got."

"Sure, sure. Don't get defensive," Murphy replied, cooling off a bit.

"I tried to dissuade them. I told them that if their daughter went missing it might be because she wanted to, but they weren't listening. I just thought they'd be better off with me than someone else. Don't worry, they'll get their money's worth."

Murphy stared at his beer. It wasn't until later that I was to find out why he was taking his involvement in the case so personally. Finally he said, "Sorry I got so worked up, but you know how it is. Something like this happens, and it can eat at a family for years. I've seen it happen before. The Smercheks are good people. Anna was a good girl. I'd hate to see it end up like that, where they spend their life savings and the rest of their lives trying to find her."

I let him stare at his beer for awhile. Finally he poured it down his throat and motioned to the bartender for another. I ordered one for myself. I figured that Murphy was going to get talkative.

"So what can you tell me about the case?"

"Not much. There's not much to tell. Anna Smercheck was a good girl. She was doing well enough in school. No drugs, sex, or alcohol that I was able to uncover. Then one day she vanishes. She never comes back to her dorm room. After a day or so, her roommate calls her parents. They hadn't heard from her. They call the police. I get the case. She had been in her last class the day she disappeared, same as usual. She didn't show up at the dining hall in her dorm, but that wasn't unusual. After seeing the food they serve, I can understand. But no one admits to seeing her after her last class."

"Were there any leads at all?"

"None that amounted to much. She didn't have a boyfriend. She didn't seem to have any close friends at the college, for that matter. There were a lot of people who knew her, even liked her in a remote sort of way, but no one she confided in."

"After I met with her parents their other daughter, Katherine, came back. She said she had left her purse, but she wanted to tell me something. She mentioned a professor named Hazeltine. Said he had some afterhours discussion group that Anna went to. Anything in that?"

"I checked Hazeltine out. It was a dead end, as far as I could find out. He's kind of an odd duck, but popular with his students. He's 'relevant' or whatever they call it these days. The only thing on his record is an arrest for disorderly conduct during a protest when he was a graduate student. I guess you can't hardly make professor now without one of those. The only link to Anna was that she was in one of his classes and went to some of his afterhours sessions, but then so did dozens of other students."

"Still, her sister seemed to think that Anna underwent some sort of change in the weeks before she went missing."

"I interviewed the sister. I wouldn't put too much faith in anything she said. She's one of those wild and imaginative types, always looking for excitement where there is none. I didn't get the impression that the two were very close."

"Probably not," I agreed.

The conversation languished. Finally I said:

"So what do you think happened to Anna?"

"God, I wish I knew," was Murphy's response. I believed he meant it. "Like I said, she just vanished. No trace, no suspects, no note, no body. Nothing to bring closure to the Smerchek's."

"You're starting to sound like some sort of social worker, Murphy." The policeman just grunted.

"You mentioned that Missing Persons was busy about the time Anna went missing."

"Nothing to it. No pattern. The other missing persons were mostly runaways, not college girls. Drifted into town, probably just drifted out. There was nothing to connect any of the cases to Anna as far as we could determine."

The bartender came by to see if we wanted another round, but Murphy waved him off.

"I've got to get going," he said as he stood up. "The missus is waiting."

I hadn't thought of Murphy as being married. Some guys get lucky, I guess.

"So there's nothing you can suggest?"

"Just poke around. See if I missed anything. If not—, well maybe make something up that will give the Smercheks some peace."

Murphy walked out of the bar looking tired. I drained my glass and followed him.

3.

My next stop was the private investigator's best friend, the public library. Murphy had made it clear I wasn't going to get access to the police records because the case was still technically active. The next best thing would be to see what the newspapers had printed at the time. Fortunately, the library kept all the back issues of both city papers on microfiche. A few minutes of sweet talking the librarian at the desk gave me a month's worth of issues of both in my hands and directions to a cubicle with a microfiche reader.

Though I hadn't remembered it as such, the story had been a nine days sensation when it broke, only fading when no new facts surfaced and the dubious activities of an alderman took up front page space.

Most of what was reported were the basic facts which agreed with what the Smercheks and Murphy had told me. Anna's roommate had called the Smercheks when Anna hadn't showed up at their dorm room two nights in a row. As far as anyone could recall, Anna had attended all of her classes the day she had disappeared. This was substantiated by the fact that there had been a quiz in her last afternoon class and the professor of that class was able to produce a quiz paper with Anna's name on it. Incidentally, she had scored a grade of 97 on the quiz, not what one would expect of someone contemplating suicide or running away.

Her student ID card had not been accessed at any of the campus dining halls that night, though one paper noted that only about half of those eligible had chosen to eat in one of those establishments that day. Anna had not had a credit card, so the police were unable to use that to trace her subsequent movements. Classmates, when questioned were unable to provide any information about her plans for the fateful evening.

The police had put out the usual appeals for information on the local radio and TV channels and a rather flattering photo of the missing girl had appeared on the front page of the evening paper.   None of this came to anything.   The few responses received by the authorities were either cases of mistaken identity or came from individuals who chronically answered such appeals, thus taking up valuable police resources.

None of Anna's classmates or acquaintances had had any hint of any change in her personality that might indicate an explanation for her disappearance. She had been, according to the papers, a model student, hard-working and academically successful. While none of those interviewed had claimed to be close to the missing girl, they all had remarked that she was friendly and likable, popular in the sort of low-key way unlikely to arouse envy, and without any known enemies. No one seemed to be aware of any romantic entanglements.

And that's about where the facts as reported in the papers ended. One paper, in the Sunday edition following the report of the disappearance, published an extensive profile of the missing girl, including information on her small town roots and her hard-working parents. Her home town was praised as the sort of place where people rarely locked their doors. The pastor at the Smerchek's church had remarked on how the missing girl had been such a lovely and caring child and how all of the congregation was praying for her safe return. The piece ended with the speculation that Anna had been unprepared for life in the big city, and in her naivety had fallen afoul of "disreputable elements." There was no evidence produced to support this conclusion, but as it fell in line with the paper's current editorial policy, it had made it into print.

After that Sunday splash, the articles became smaller and were to be found in the back pages. Finally they were reduced to short notices stating that the police had uncovered no new clues and anyone with information should contact the authorities.

In what was obviously an attempt to revive flagging interest in what had initially showed promise as a sensational story, the following Sunday saw yet another lengthy piece, this one dealing with missing persons cases in general and what sort of pitfalls faced young women in modern society.

I read this one with interest, hoping that it might reveal something of a pattern or similarity amongst the other missing persons cases. Unfortunately, the reporter had been long on speculation and short on details. There had been, as Murphy had mentioned, an uptick in the number of missing persons cases reported. However, most of those had been resolved as the usual string of runaways or drug abuse victims. There had been no rash of bodies turning up in isolated places. Most of the cases were juveniles, few of whom could be described as model students or caring children.

After that, the story disappeared from the papers. I spent another fruitless hour combing the paper for any sort of related story, but found nothing that seemed to be related. The police reports for the period preceding and following the disappearance produced their occasional amusing anecdotes, but if there was a tie-in to Anna Smerchek it wasn't one that I could discover.

I collected up the microfiche and returned them to the desk neatly arranged in chronological order. I have always found that it paid off in my line of work to stay on good terms with the library staff. On a hunch, I asked her if there was any information available about Professor Hazeltine. She pointed me towards several references. As an afterthought, she mentioned that she seemed to remember that the university magazine had had an article about the professor sometime in the last few years. Fortunately, the library had back issues available in the periodical stacks if I cared to search for it. I thanked her for being most helpful.

The first reference the librarian had suggested provided the dates and institutions of the professor's various degrees, the dates of his various academic appointments including his current position as tenured professor at the university. I don't know much about that kind of thing, but at least I recognized the names of the schools he had attended as being legitimate institutions.

The second reference contained a list of the professor's publications. Most of these were in what I assumed were academic journals and had titles such as "Shakespeare and the influence of pre-Elizabethan Playwrights." A few had more unusual subject matter, "The Vampyre in Literature," being among the more notable. It also appeared that the professor wrote the occasional article for less academic periodicals. These tended to have more sensational titles featuring zombies, werewolves, and vampires. It appeared that Hazeltine was something of an authority on the subject. It appeared that he had also written a popular book on the subject. I consulted the card catalog, found that the library did have a copy, but when I looked for it on the shelves it appeared that it had been checked out.

That left the university magazine, a glossy production that mostly seemed geared towards inspiring alumni contributions. The article in question turned out to have been published two and a half years earlier, but I did find the issue containing it.

The article, itself, praised the Hazeltine as a popular professor of pre-modern European literature. There was a picture showing him lecturing to a packed house in one of the larger lecture halls. His academic background was fleshed out from what I had found in the references, but basically covered the same territory. It also mentioned his popular works, and it appeared that there were two, not just the one. It also appeared that he had been a consultant on a Hollywood thriller, *"Blood of the Vampyre's Daughter"* which according to the article had been a critical success but a box office failure. His first and second year literature courses were popular and his upper class courses were well regarded. He seemed to be a minor authority on pre-Elizabethan plays. There was a brief paragraph towards the end of the article about his afterhours sessions where, as the article put it, "more esoteric topics were often discussed." All in all, the professor came off as something of a character, but not necessarily one possessing the attributes of a prime suspect.

On my way out, I thanked the woman at the desk politely, assured her that she had been most helpful. She, for her part, invited me to come back any time. I bid her a pleasant good night and left.

As I walked to my car, I went over in my mind what I had found out. It turned out not to be much. The only thing that struck me was that the stories, minus some minor journalistic excesses, of the Smercheks, Murphy, and the newspapers were in remarkable agreement. But the story they told didn't add up to a disappearing girl.

In that story, Anna Smerchek was not the sort of girl who you would expect to run away. There were none of the usual elements that you see in disappearances, no sex, drugs, or money problems. No one seemed to think she did drugs. There had been no mention of any sort of boyfriend, or girlfriend for that matter. And somehow, I couldn't see Anna Smerchek owing money to a loan shark or the mob.

Unfortunately, the only theory that seemed to fit the story was that Anna Smerchek had been picked up off the street in a random act and whisked away, either to a life of white slavery or to a shallow grave. But that just seemed to melodramatic. I knew that things like that did happen occasionally, but much less often than bad novels would lead you to suspect. When such things happened in real life, there tended to be some sort of connection, however tenuous, between the victim and their kidnapper.

So where did that leave me? It seemed the one solid lead that I had, the one line of investigation which I could pursue and actually give the Smercheks something for their money was this Professor Hazeltine. It seemed a long shot, but my next step seemed like it would have to be an interview with the professor.

4.

Professor Hazeltine's office was buried on the third floor of the building that housed most of the Humanities Department and was known to most people as the Humanities Building, though in fact it had been named after some long forgotten benefactor who had paid for its construction. It had been built around the turn of the century in a style best described as "red brick castle." It was starting to look a little worn these days, but I had to admit it had a certain academic charm lacking in the more recent examples of campus architecture.

The prime offices on the third floor were on the outside walls and had tall, narrow windows. The less illustrious or less senior staff were housed in interior chambers illuminated only by dingy globes hanging from the high ceiling and whatever light made it through the transoms over the doors. Professor Hazeltine was to be found in one of these, Room 313. I wondered if the number was an omen.

The door was open when I found it, 313 painted in cracked black lettering on the frosted pane of the door. The professor's name was printed on a card that fit into a frame on the wall next to the door. I knocked on the door to get Hazeltine's attention.

The professor responded with "Come in." He was seated at an ancient oak desk pushed against the back wall. Most of the rest of the office was taken up by bookcases filled to overflowing with an assortment of books, pamphlets, and papers. The professor himself looked the perfect image of what a professor should look like in the public's eye, at least a public basing their ideas on 1930's movies. Dr. Hazeltine was a short, slender man with thinning hair and thick glasses. He was wearing a tweed jacket complete with leather elbow patches. Despite the prominent "No Smoking" signs in the corridors there was a briar pipe sitting on his desk next to a pouch of tobacco. He didn't strike me as exactly the kind of heartthrob a young coed might fall for.

"We talked on the phone, Professor Hazeltine."

"Yes. You said you were a private investigator." The last was halfway between a statement and a question.

"Yes. I'm investigating the disappearance of Anna Smerchek. On behalf of her family."

"Yes, something of a mystery. And a tragedy if anything has happened to her. She was a bright young girl. But I thought the police were already investigating the case."

"They are. But you understand that the police have limited resources and more than one case to occupy their efforts. The family has asked me to look into the matter to see if I can find any trace of their daughter."

"I see," Hazeltine said with a certain amount of reticence. "You'll have to forgive me. I haven't had dealings with a private detective before. I had sort of assumed they were mostly a myth. Something out of fiction, like vampires and werewolves."

"I assure you I'm real. I can show you my license if you would like."

"Oh, that won't be necessary. What can I do for you?"

"I understand that Anna was a student of yours?"

"Yes, she was in my Pre-Modern World Literature class last year. That's a freshman survey class. I teach it with a colleague. He covers the classics in the fall term and then I take over in the spring term. We cover snippets of everything from Gilgamesh to The Spanish Tragedie, with brief stops at Homer, Virgil, Beowulf , and some translations of Chinese, Indian and Japanese works. She did quite well in it. I gave her an A. As I said, she was a bright girl."

"She went missing in late October, or at least that's the last anyone remembers seeing her. When did this course end?" I asked.

"At the end of the Spring term last year. Finals were right before Memorial Day."

"And that was the last you saw of her?"

"No. She wasn't in any of my classes this year, but I did see her several times around campus during the fall term this year."

"I understand that she also attended some sort of afterhours seminar of yours?"

"You seem particularly well informed," Hazeltine remarked somewhat acidly. "It's not so much a seminar as an informal discussion group. No credits are given and participation is whoever happens to show up for a particular session. We usually hold it in a room in the Student Union if one is available. Otherwise we just try to find a quiet corner somewhere. It's not a big group, usually only a dozen or so students show up."

"And Anna was one of those?"

"For a while. I issue an open invitation at the start of the term in each of my classes. Anna started coming sometime in February I think. She came regularly during the spring term last year and for the first few sessions this fall and but then she stopped coming. That's often the case. People drop in for a bit and then find other interests—"

"If you don't mind my asking, professor, exactly what kind of things were discussed in these discussion groups?"

"Oh the topics would vary from week to week, but the purpose of the group was to explore the odd corners of literature, things that aren't ordinarily covered in the official curriculum. Works that everyone has heard of, but no one has read. It's meant to be fun while broadening the students view of the world. I usually suggest some texts and topics at the start of a term and then things evolve from there. Sometimes I'll ask one of my colleagues to give a short talk on a particular subject they are interested in."

"You said that you cover the odd corners of literature. I'm not quite sure I understand what you mean by that, professor. Could you give me some examples?"

"Well, one topic that always proves popular is vampires. Everyone has seen them in the movies, but far fewer have read Bram Stoker's Dracula let alone some of the older texts that he based his work on. I try to get the students to explore the original literature. We usually do werewolves, too. Zombies have been popular of late, as well."

"I see. What does the university think of these seminars?"

"As I said, the whole thing is very informal. I don't think the university really cares. It's similar to some of the film clubs on campus.   For example, there is one of the film groups that specializes in horror movies.   I know a few students who participate in both groups.   I must say, I'm not sure what all this has to do with Anna's disappearance.   It's almost as if you suspect me."

"It's not that, professor.   I'm just trying to get into the mind of Anna Smerchek.   Something seems to have happened to her around the middle of the fall term this year.   Her personality took a shift.   Her letters to home changed in tone, then stopped.   I'm thinking if I can figure out what caused that change, maybe I can find some trace of where she went.   Or at least what happened to her."

"You don't think she's still alive, do you?"

"I'm not hopeful.   Of course kids run away all the time, but Anna doesn't seem to fit that profile.   She was a bright student with friends, got along well with her family.   Even when kids like that do run away, they usually reappear in a week or two."

"I want you to know I'm a concerned as anyone.   I liked Anna. I wouldn't want anything to have happen to her."

"I'm sure you don't, professor."

"Look, if you think the discussion group is somehow involved why don't you come to the next session?   It's tomorrow night, in fact, at eight, in the student union.   Some of the attendees knew Anna better that I did.   Maybe they can help.   And I'm sure the rest will be more than thrilled to meet a real live private eye."

"I just might take you up on that, professor."

As I left the Humanities building I had to admit to myself that I didn't quite know what to make of Professor Hazeltine.   He had seemed open enough, not at all like someone with something to hide.   There certainly wasn't anything menacing about his personality.   He hadn't seemed nervous under my questioning, either.   Despite the fact that we had little in common, I found myself wanting to like the guy.

On the surface he didn't seem to be the type of teacher that would cause young women to fawn over him.   He certainly didn't have that sort of dashing aura about him that would allow him to seduce his female students. On the contrary, he came across as rather nerdish, a man caught in the stereotypes of his own undergraduate days. If he were really interested in bedding young women, you'd have thought he would have made some effort to appear more hip. Of course, I could be completely off base. Maybe there was a faction of women who would find that sort of intellectuality appealing. I've never claimed to understand women of any age, and my own life has never been marked by success with the other sex.

On the other hand, from what I had read, Hazeltine was an extremely popular lecturer. His courses at any level were always full. While his academic credentials were sound enough to have secured him tenure, he also seemed to have been able to hone in on the pop-culture trends that appealed to his students. Did that extend to being able to manipulate them for his own ends? I didn't know, but by attending one of his afterhours sessions as he had suggested, I might be able to find out, or at least determine if he had tendencies in that direction.

5.

I thought that as long as I was on campus I might as well try to interview some of Anna's acquaintances. I knew the dormitory and name of her roommate from the information that the Smerchek's had given me. I managed to get the directions to the former after several attempts at questioning self absorbed students. It turned out to be one of the newer buildings, a stark, modernistic tower of eight or ten stories that had nothing whatsoever to recommend it architecturally.

The ground floor was given over to an open lounge area that seemed to have been designed to provide clear views of all its corners to the person manning the "Information" desk. This latter served as a gateway to the elevators leading up to the upper floor. The intention seemed to be to keep unauthorized individuals, such as myself, from disturbing the students while they were doing whatever college students do these days.

Fortunately for my purposes, the person manning the desk was a rather cheerfully happy coed. While there was no way that she was going to allow me to proceed to the higher floors, she did offer me the use of a house phone and room directory. In the latter, I found a listing for an Anna Smerchek and a Betsy Williams, room 617. I was in luck. My call to that room was answered by Williams and with a little persuading, she agreed to come down to the lounge to meet me. Under the rather skeptical eye of the information desk, who had overheard my end of the conversation, I took a seat on one of the rather uncomfortable blue vinyl sofas facing the elevators.

A few minutes later a young woman emerged from the elevator and looked around the lounge with a somewhat puzzled expression. I assumed that this was Betsy Williams.

"Miss Williams?" I asked.

She gave me a rather dubious once over. Not that I could blame her under the circumstances.

"You said you wanted to ask some questions about Anna?" she asked in a surprisingly self-assured voice. In some ways, Betsy Williams fit perfectly the stereotype of a college coed. She was dressed in slightly ragged blue jeans, a shapeless sweater and low heeled shoes. She had brown, shoulder length hair pulled back in a careless pony tail and wore no detectable makeup. If the black rimmed glasses were intended to make her look studious, they certainly succeeded, but when I studied the eyes behind them I saw the light of intelligence and perhaps a bit of a sense of humor. She wasn't pretty in a superficial way, but I got the feeling that someday she would break some young man's heart.

"Yes. I'm a private investigator. Anna's parents have hired me to look into her disappearance. I've got a letter from them explaining that." I produced the form I had had them sign in my office as well as my P.I. license. She studied both of them carefully, for what I'm not sure. Anyone could have whipped up the letter with a few minutes at a typewriter and, as a document, my license doesn't look like much or mean much either. It did have a bad photo of me, which only proved that I was the person in the photo. After a moment she handed back the papers and suggested that we move over to a seating group, that while out of earshot of the information desk was still in clear view. It seemed that Betsy Williams was a very sensible young lady.

"You were Anna's roommate?" I asked when we were seated.

"Yes," Betsy answered tersely.

"Was that last year as well?"

"Yes. Neither one of us knew anyone that was going to school here, so we were just assigned to each other as freshmen. It seemed to work out okay, so we decided to stay roommates this year."

"That makes sense. Is there anything that you can tell me about Anna that might explain her disappearance?"

"No. I was as surprised as anyone when she didn't come back to the room that night. I didn't think too much about it at the time. I had gone to bed fairly early because I had an early class the next morning. I just thought that Anna was studying late in the library or out with some people she knew. When I got up in the morning, I just thought she was taking a shower or something, and I headed out to class right away. She hadn't made her bed the day before, which wasn't unusual. Neither one of us are neat freaks. That's one of the reasons we got along so well. It wasn't until she didn't turn up later that I realized something was wrong. That's when I called her parents."

"So she hadn't said anything about her plans that night?"

"No. I explained all that when the police questioned me," she said brusquely.

"Unfortunately, I don't have access to the police files, Miss Williams. I'm afraid I may have to cover a lot of the same ground."

That seemed to mollify her a bit.

"Had she given any hints of problems previous to her disappearance? Boyfriend issues maybe, or problems with her courses?"

"No. She was doing well as far as her grades went. At least she didn't seem worried. And as far as I know, she didn't have any regular boyfriend."

"Oh?"

"You have to understand that we weren't what you could call close. We got along well as roommates because we had similar habits. Neither one of us were big on partying. We both took are studies seriously, kept similar hours. But we tended not to pry into each other's private lives such as they were. Sure, we'd go out for pizza or something together occasionally, or hit a movie, but we didn't hang around with each other that much."

"What about classes? Did you have many classes together?"

"None. That's not surprising. I'm a math major. Anna hadn't settled on a major yet, but she was much more a liberal artsy sort. I thought she'd end up as an Anthropology or History major. Something like that. As freshmen we didn't even take the same literature class."

"I guess I don't know much about college, Miss Williams."

"Everyone has to take a literature class freshman year. It's supposed to make us well rounded or something. I took Modern

American, Anna took Pre-Modern World Lit. As for the rest of my schedule it was Calculus, Physics and Chemistry. Anna took a history class, a science for non-science majors and business math. I had to help her with both of those. She just wasn't into math or science."

"But you said she got good grades."

"Sure. She was bright and worked hard. And the fact is the standards for those kind of courses aren't that high."

"Out of curiosity, how are your grades?"

She looked surprised and then a little annoyed. "I get straight A's if you must know. I don't see that it's relevant."

"Perhaps not. I'm sorry if I've offended you. I just like to know something about the people I interview. It helps me judge how much I can trust what they say."

"And me? Can you trust what I say?"

"I can assure you, Miss Williams, I'm confident you are being both accurate and truthful." That seemed to settle her down a bit. "What about her friends? Did you know any of them?"

"I'm not sure that Anna had any real close friends. She seemed to get along with everybody, and there were people in her classes that she would study with or do things with sometimes, but no one that she was close with. And as I said earlier, if she had a boyfriend, she was keeping it a secret."

"Do you think that was possible? That she was keeping a relationship a secret, I mean. Maybe because she was having an affair with an older man? A professor?"

"I don't think so. She didn't show any of the signs."

"Signs?"

"You can tell when someone is in love, or at least thinks they are. They get distracted, preoccupied. Disappear unexpectedly. Anna didn't do any of that—" Then it caught her, "except, of course for when she did."

"You mentioned she took the Pre-Modern World Literature course. Do you know of a Professor Hazeltine?"

"Sure. He's something of a campus celebrity. His courses are wildly popular, probably because he talks about things like zombies and werewolves. I don't know if anyone takes him seriously, though."

"Did Anna ever talk about him?"

"Sure. She talked about all her professors, we both did. She liked his class. I gather that he's a very entertaining lecturer."

"I understand that he holds afterhours sessions, and that Anna went to some of them."

"Yeah. She talked about them, sometimes. Again, the occult pop-culture kind of thing. I'm not really interested in that sort of nonsense."

"What sort of nonsense are you interested in?"

"Number theory, fractals, topological manifolds."

"I take it that's all math nonsense?"

"Yes." She actually smiled.

"I understand she stopped going to those sessions a few weeks before she disappeared. Do you have any idea why?"

"Probably because she was busy," Betsy answered. "You don't think there was something between Professor Hazeltine and Anna, do you? I didn't ever get the impression she thought of him in that way. He is kind of funny looking, you know."

"Yes. I've met the professor." I suppose to a twenty year old all men over forty look funny. "Did you notice any change in Anna's mood in the weeks before she disappeared?"

"No, not really. Maybe she was a little more serious, a little more withdrawn. But I just thought it was because she was busy with her studies."

"Is there anything else you can think of that might be helpful? Anyone I should talk to?"

"No, I'm afraid not," she replied. It denial seemed very genuine. "Can I ask you what you think happened to Anna?"

"You can ask, but I'm afraid I don't have any answers yet. The case seems atypical. As far as I've discovered so far, Anna wasn't the type that usually runs away or disappears."

"Do you think she's still alive?"

"I really couldn't say. I noticed during our conversation that you kept referring to her in the past tense—"

"I just have a feeling—"

"I know what you mean. I want to thank you for your time, Miss Williams. You've been very helpful."

We stood up and shook hands. I gave her one of my cards and told her to give me a call if anything came to her. She went back up the elevator to her room while I left under the watchful eye of the information desk.

6.

I dressed casually for Hazeltine's session the next night, tweed jacket over a dark turtleneck sweater and jeans, which shows you how much I knew about current campus fashions. Except for the fact that I hadn't had a haircut in a month, I still looked like a cop, or at least an ex-cop.

The professor hadn't given me specific directions, just that the session was in the student union at eight. The student union was a big, rambling building that had been built in a vaguely beaux arts style sometime in the twenties and added on to several times since. When I walked up the massive front steps and passed into the entry hall I realized I was hopelessly loss. Fortunately, I found the information desk where the coed on duty was able to provide me directions. I was discovering that there actually were a lot of people at the university who were willing to be helpful. It was kind of refreshing.

Hazeltine's session was being held in a small lounge on the third floor. I made my way up the central staircase. Halfway between the second and third floor my knee realized that it would have been happier taking the elevator. I paused a moment to lean on the railing, then continued up to the third floor.

The lounge proved to be a well lit room painted a cheerful yellow. An assortment of couches and chairs were scattered around. What I assume were paintings by students were hung on the wall, at least I hoped they had been done by students. If not, somebody's money was going to waste.

There were about a dozen students already there, all but two of whom were male. They were dressed about what you'd expect of students, jeans and sweatshirts mostly. One guy was dressed in shorts and sandals despite the fact that there were still traces of snow on the ground outside. Hair was mostly shaggy and shaving was obviously optional, though only a couple of them could be said to have actual beards. The youngest looked like he might have been fifteen, but was probably older, most looked to be around twenty. There was one guy sitting in the corner who was about six four and two-fifty, all muscle, that looked a little older. He was carrying on a conversation with the fifteen year old and smiling, which I thought was probably a good sign.

Professor Hazeltine was at the back of the room chatting up one of the two women. She was maybe twenty-one, with long blonde hair pulled back in a thick braid. She was kind of skinny, but other than that not bad looking.

The professor noticed me as I walked into the room and motioned me over.

"I'm glad you could make it. We're just about ready to get started. It might be best if you just watched for a while. I'll introduce you later, maybe let you answer a few questions and then you can go into you purpose for coming."

"That sounds alright," I responded. I grabbed an unoccupied seat where I could watch most of the room.

Hazeltine got up and made a short speech. A few stragglers came in while he was talking, but no one seemed to notice. It seemed as though everyone had been to these sessions before and knew what to expect.

The professor introduced the topic which turned out to be werewolves. The discussion veered to which werewolf movies were everybody's favorite. Hazeltine let the discussion run for a while without interrupting and then he asked how many had read Bram Stoker's play. About half of those present raised their hands. They talked about that for awhile and then someone mentioned some guy named Vlad Tepische or something like that.

Hazeltine was doing a pretty good job of keeping the discussion going without saying too much himself. From what I could tell, the students were enjoying the conversation without taking it too seriously. After about an hour the talk started to wind down and people began repeating themselves. At that point the professor took control again.

"As an added bonus tonight, we have an opportunity to talk with a creature nearly as mythological as werewolves, a real, genuine private investigator."

This seemed to get everyone's attention. The guy with the muscles straightened up in his seat. He'd taken off the leather jacket he'd been wearing. I could see what looked like a Marine Corp. logo tattooed where his right bicep bulged out under his black T-shirt.

Hazeltine gave me an introduction and then opened things up for questions. There were all the usual things that people ask you when they find out you're a P.I., how I came to be a private detective, did I carry a gun, that sort of thing. The guy in the shorts asked if I had a beautiful secretary and seemed disappointed when I said no. I tried to answer the questions truthfully. The conversation wandered off to what I thought of detective novels. I said I didn't read many, but I found them mostly unrealistic. Police procedurals I just found depressing.

Finally, Hazeltine interrupted the discussion and let me state my business.

"I've been hired by the family of Anna Smerchek to investigate her disappearance. If any of you know anything that might be helpful, I'd appreciate hearing about it."

They started talking about Anna. Only about half of them knew her either from the sessions or classes. Everybody seemed to think she was a nice girl but somewhat reserved. No one had been particularly close to her. In short, it was pretty much the same picture that I'd gotten from her roommate and the papers.

I thanked them and handed out business cards in case anyone remembered anything useful. After that, things kind of broke up and people started to put on their jackets and leave.

I stood around for a moment not sure what to do.

"Not very helpful, I take it?" Hazeltine asked.

"Considering I wasn't expecting much, it was okay. I'm still trying to understand Anna. From what everyone has told me, she was friendly enough but not really close to anyone."

"There are a lot of students like that, I think," Hazeltine commented. "The whole college experience kind of overwhelms them. They're so busy with classes and they meet so many new people all at once that they never really form deep relationships with anyone. That's particularly true at a big institution like this."

"Yeah. I wouldn't know. I never went to college."

"You might have missed something."

"Probably. But I got drafted right out of high school. After that, the Police Academy. Then I got shot. Not much time for anything in between."

"Got time for a beer?"

"Is it close?" It was getting late and I was tired.

"Two floors down. The Union Commons sells beer to students and faculty that are of age."

It seemed that Hazeltine was trying to be a regular guy. Maybe he was, I thought, or maybe he was trying to play me. Either way having a beer with him might not be a bad idea.

"Sure, why not."

The Commons was a large room on the main floor filled with tables and chairs. At one end there was a low stage, but that was empty. The room probably hadn't changed much since the place had been built. Groups of students were scattered around the room, some pretending to study, some playing cards, some just talking. Rock music was playing over the sound system, not loud enough to be deafening, but loud enough to cause you to speak up. Beer in plastic cups could be found on many of the tables. The place hadn't been designed for clear sight lines, there were plenty of nooks and crannies providing privacy. Hazeltine led me to a table in one of these and then said he'd be back with beer.

I looked around while I waited. What I saw was about what you'd expect. Kids mostly, late teens, early twenties with a few older types intermingled. Faculty, graduate students, students who had been out in the real world for a few years? It was hard to tell. The sex ratio seemed to be about even in the part of the room that I could see. The preppie look was definitely out, but most of the people I could see were reasonably clean if a bit shaggy. It didn't look like a dangerous environment.

My musings were interrupted by Hazeltine's return with a couple of sixteen ounce cups of beer.

"I'm sorry that tonight wasn't more productive for you," Hazeltine said.

"It was about what I expected. Most police work is like that. You ask a lot of questions and most of the time the answers don't mean anything. Police work is not like what you read in cheap paperback novels. Or even the good ones. Mostly it's routine, covering all the bases, hoping for the one clue that gives you a handle on the case."

"You miss being a policeman, don't you?"

"I must, otherwise I'd get an easier job that paid more."

We both took a sip of our beers.

"You really think she's dead, don't you?" Hazeltine asked. It was more of a statement than a question. He was right, though.

"Yeah, probably. After this long she'd probably have turned up if she was still alive."

"Do the police think I'm a suspect?" The question that had been lurking since I'd met the professor was out in the open.

"I don't know what the police think. They don't tell me what's on their mind anymore."

"Alright. Fair enough. Do you consider me a suspect?"

I looked at the professor. His face was in the shadows, but there was enough light to read his expression. It wasn't one of fear, but Hazeltine was worried.

"Yeah. Maybe." That was the answer he'd expected, even if it wasn't the one he wanted to hear.

"Look, professor. It's nothing personal. It's just that in a case like this cops play the percentages. Most often it's someone in the family or a close family friend. That doesn't seem to be the case, here. The father was working in his hardware store the day Anna disappeared. Same thing the day before and the day after. That was one of the first things the police checked. Sure he might have driven down after work, but it's a three hour drive here and back. His absence would have been noted. No one else from up there seems a likely suspect, either."

"After the family, you start to think neighbors, boyfriends, that kind of thing. She lived in a dorm and no one seems to have known about any boyfriends. Or girl friends for that matter. Next you look at authority figures in her life, clergy, doctors, teachers. I'm afraid that's where you come in. From what we know Anna went to Sunday services but wasn't otherwise active in the church down here. She hadn't been to a doctor down here, either. So that leaves teachers. Let's face it, professor, you're kind of a charismatic figure on campus, the kind of person that might be able to influence an impressionable young woman."

"I didn't do it. You've got to believe me."

"I didn't say you did, professor. But until you can be eliminated, I'm afraid you are a prime suspect. Of course, if you didn't do it, you probably don't have anything to worry about."

"Look. I want to find out what happened to Anna as much as anyone. I liked her. She was a good student. Better than a good student; she was really interested in literature. Not that I wouldn't feel the same about any other of my students, even the ones flunking out. But it's more than that. I know the police haven't charged me or anything, but people around here aren't stupid." Considering where we were, his statement was ironic. "They know she was a student of mine, and they can guess that I'm on a short list of suspects. Even a hint of scandal can ruin the career of a man in my position. And given my interest in unusual topics, well—"

I looked the professor over. What I saw was a worried man, but not one in a panic.

"Just what are you saying, professor?"

"I guess what I'm saying is that if there is anything that I can do to help resolve Anna's disappearance, all you have to do is ask."

That wasn't quite what I had expected. Hazeltine seemed sincere in his offer. Of course, if he was involved he could just be trying to keep close so he'd know what was going on. But I didn't think so.

"I'll keep that in mind, professor."

Hazeltine finished what was left of his beer in one big swallow. "I mean it. You have my office number. Here's my home phone."

He handed me a card with a phone number on it.

"It's getting late. I have to get going." The professor stood and nervously held out his hand. I took it.

"Thanks for the beer, professor. It's been an interesting night."

7.

I was almost out of the student union when a young man came up to me. I recognized him as one of the students that had attended the session that night, though he hadn't said much. Except for a surplus fatigue jacket that was several sizes too large, he was reasonably neat and presentable. He was also very nervous.

"You were at the session tonight, weren't you?" I said in what I hoped was a friendly tone of voice. "Did you know Anna?"

"Yes. That's what I'd like to talk to you about, if you've got a moment."

"I'm all ears." There were a couple of chairs in an alcove off of the lobby that looked reasonably private, so I said, "Why don't we sit over there."

"OK." He took one of the chairs, scrunching himself down in his jacket.

There's an art to interviewing a witness who is teetering between not saying anything and spilling his guts. I'm not sure that I've ever mastered it, but mostly it involves being patient. It looked like I was going to need to exercise that patience.

"You knew Anna, then? Were you her boyfriend?"

"No." It seemed his vocabulary had dried up with his courage.

I took a shot in the dark. "But you wanted to be, didn't you?"

He looked surprised at my statement, but I could see that I had hit the mark.

"Yeah. Kind of, at least. I'd asked her out to a movie at the film society. It was one of the horror flicks that had come up at one Professor Hazeltine's sessions."

"Did she accept?"

"Yes."

"And what happened?"

"What do you mean what happened?" he asked, suddenly defensive.

"Well, did you go to the movie? Did she like it? Did you do anything afterwards?"

"Yeah, we went to the movie. It was alright, I guess. Maybe a little silly."

"And after the movie?

"I walked her back to her dorm. She said she had an early class the next day." It wasn't much of a confession, but I felt more sympathy for the kid.

"When was this?"

"I don't know. About the middle of September. A couple of weeks after classes started."

"So the two of you went to a movie and you walked her home. Nothing wrong with that. But that isn't what you wanted to tell me, is it?"

"No, I guess not."

"What did you want to tell me?"

"Look, I really liked Anna. She was nice, she was smart—" He hesitated.

"Attractive?" I supplied.

"Yes."

"And—?"

"Well, I wanted to impress her."

"Natural enough," I replied with a smile. "So how were you going to do that?"

"I'd heard about this place. It's called the House of Esoteric Wisdom. It's kind of a book shop. I knew from Professor Hazeltine's sessions that she was interested in the occult, magic, things like that—"

"Oh?" No one that had been interviewed by the police or the newspapers had mentioned that. Even Hazeltine seemed to have been unaware of any interest in the topic.

"I don't mean that she was into black magic or anything like that. But she was intrigued by the unusual. Coming from a little town up north I don't think she'd been exposed much to things like that. Even the fact that I was Jewish seemed exotic to her."

The kid didn't look particularly Jewish to me, but then his religion hadn't seemed particularly important.

"So where does this House of Esoteric Wisdom come in?"

"The guy that runs it gives lectures. On 'esoteric wisdom' whatever that is. I talked Anna into going to one of them. I thought she'd find it interesting."

"Did she?"

"Maybe. I'm not sure."

"So the two of you went to one of these lectures. When was this?"

"It was about a week and a half after the movie."

"So, about the beginning of October?"

"Yeah. I guess so."

"And what happened?"

"Not much. I thought the 'lecture' was a bunch of crap, myself. A lot of it was about expanding the power of the individual. There was a bunch of mystical and astrological stuff that I thought was nonsense."

"What did Anna think?"

"I don't really know. She didn't say anything afterwards. But when I talked to her a few days later she was—well different." That, at least, fit in with what others had said about the girl, that a change had come over her around the beginning of October.

"And you think that something Anna heard at this lecture might have been the cause?"

He shook his head uncertainly. "I just don't know. Like I said, it just seemed a bunch of nonsense to me. I don't see how anyone could have taken it seriously."

"What about the lecturer? What was he like?"

"Kind of creepy, actually. He's this tall, thin guy. Long black hair swept back. Dresses in black, and I don't just mean black jeans and t-shirt. It's like an outfit. He speaks with an accent, too, sort of middle-European. More like Bela Lugosi, really. I couldn't tell if it was real or just a put-on."

"Did he say anything in particular to you or Anna?"

"Well, there were only maybe a half-dozen people at this lecture. Of the girls, Anna was by far the best looking. This guy, I think his name was Romanescu or something like that, was interested in her. After the lecture was over he came up to us, asked us what we thought, said we were welcome to come back. It was pretty clear he was a lot more interested in Anna coming back than me."

"What happened then?"

"We left. I walked Anna back to her dorm."

"I see. Did you go out with Anna after that?"

"No. I asked a couple of times, but she said she was busy. It wasn't like we were really dating or a couple or anything, so I didn't think too much of it at the time. Then she went missing—"

"Yeah. Why didn't you mention this to the police? You didn't, did you?"

"No. I didn't think it was important at first. This happened nearly a month before Anna disappeared. Romanescu just seemed kind of creepy to me. I guess, though, I could see how he might hold a fascination for a woman. There was something about his eyes that kind of drew you in, but I didn't think he was the sort of guy Anna would fall for. That's why I didn't mention it to anybody. Besides, I didn't want to get involved. If it turned out I was the one who introduced her to—"

"—to whoever killed her," I finished.

"Yeah."

"So you think Anna is dead, too?"

"Yeah." It was clear the kid was feeling a lot of guilt. "Well, like I said, I didn't want to get involved. My parents would kill me. They'd probably kill me just for being interested in a Gentile."

"Parents can be like that." Part of me wanted to tell the kid that if he'd spoken up earlier, Anna might still be alive, but I didn't want him to clam up. Part of me was just sorry for him. "Why are you telling me all this now?"

"I'm not sure. I guess it's been eating at me. When you showed up tonight, well— I just had to speak up."

"You're doing the right thing. You know you might have to repeat your story to the police at some point?"

"Do I have to?"

"Maybe. It depends on what happens. In any case, you'd better give me your name and where I can get in touch with you."

He pulled out a pad of paper and wrote his name down on it.

"While you're at it, put down the address of this 'House of Esoteric Wisdom,' too. I think I'll need to check it out."

"You won't tell the cops unless you have to, will you?"

I couldn't tell whether he was more afraid of the police or his parents. "Not unless it seems necessary. I wouldn't worry about. They might give you a hard time about not coming forth earlier, but they don't usually go spreading the names of witnesses around unless they have to testify."

"Thanks. I guess I better get going." He zipped up his jacket and left.

I followed him down the steps of the Union. It might be the end of March, but there was a cold, damp wind blowing. I thought about what the kid had told me. He had seemed honest enough. Honest enough to feel guilt. I didn't think he was responsible for what had happened to Anna. But that wouldn't stop the guilty feelings from haunting him when she was finally discovered.

8.

The House of Esoteric Wisdom was in an older residential neighborhood not far from the campus. Most of the houses on the street had been built around the turn of the century at a time when families had been large and servants had been common. They had originally been occupied by members of the middle class of that era, professional men, successful businessmen, perhaps even a few of the professors at the university. Inevitably, over the years they had become less fashionable, less practical, and too large and expensive to maintain as single family residences. Most of them had been subdivided into flats and apartments largely catering to students and other short term renters and had taken on an aura of shabby carelessness.

The building that had become The House of Esoteric Wisdom was a two story frame structure of the form called a four-square because it was essentially cubical in shape. The hip-roofed attic space had large projecting dormers on at least the front and sides, and judging from the curtains drawn across the dormer's windows, probably was occupied. A wide covered porch took up most of the frontage. The house had recently been painted white, and looked to be in no better or worse condition than its neighbors.

A sign proclaiming it as "The House of Esoteric Wisdom" hung over the broad steps leading up to the porch. The letters were in red on a black background that looked out of place against the white paint of the house. I mounted the steps, giving my leg a moment to rest once I was on the porch deck and took a look around. There were a couple of battered wicker chairs with faded cushions and the remains of a potted plant that had succumbed over the winter. A large window in the room which originally must have been the parlor held another "House of Esoteric Wisdom" sign as well as a collection of books on astrology and magic. The front door held a sign that said "OPEN". I took the hint and entered.

There was one of those bell things that rang as I walked through the front door. It took me a moment to adjust to the gloomy interior after the bright sun outside. I found myself in a large entry hall with a wide staircase leading up to the second floor. Everywhere I looked there was dark woodwork and darker wallpaper all lit by one chandelier with several missing bulbs hanging from above. The room to the left, the parlor, seemed to have been converted into a book store, the room to the right, presumably the original dining room, had a number of mismatched folding chairs set up facing what might be construed as either a lectern or an altar, depending on how you looked at it. Obviously the place where Romanescu gave his spiel.

I turned into the book store and pretended to browse under the gaze of the girl behind the counter. She was rail thin with long straight hair that had been bleached white and she wore a floor-length, high-necked black dress. The pale tone of her skin might charitably have been ascribed to the fact that it was the end of a long, bleak winter. She had chosen to enhance it with a lipstick shade that might have been black or a very, very dark red and matched the polish on her long pointed nails. If you've seen a cheap horror movie, you get the idea.

The books on display echoed those in the window, astrology, magic, witchcraft. A lot of it even I knew was junk, but there did seem to be some volumes by Waite and Crowley put out by obscure publishers of the occult. The glass display case behind which the clerk stood contained an assortment of black candles, cheap jewelry in the shape of anhks and other supposedly mystic symbols, and jars containing what might or might not be herbs.

"Can I help you?" The tone indicated that assistance was the last thing on her mind.

"Don't mind me. I'm just browsing. I'll let you know if I find something I'm interested in."

I continued poking around the shop. Judging from the prices and the fact that I was the only customer, there was no way that the place was even breaking even. Even granting that things were slow because it was early afternoon, the place wasn't a viable business. It had to be a front of some sort. The question was a front for what? Drugs? Sex? It certainly wasn't rock and roll.

The shop girl seemed to be getting uneasy at my presence. Finally she spoke up. "How did you find out about the House?" She said it like that, capitalized.

"Oh, I think a friend of mine mentioned it. Maybe you know her? Her name is Anna, Anna Smerchek."

If I had expected to get a reaction, I'd have been disappointed. The name hadn't triggered any sort of recognition on her part. The question had, however, increased her nervousness.

"If you'll excuse me for a moment, I have to check on something." She disappeared through a beaded curtain that hung over the doorway from the parlor to some other room towards the back of the house.

I could hear the sound of low voices, too muffled to understand the words though the tone was clear enough, then the girl came back. A moment later she was followed by a man that fit the description the kid had given me of Romanescu.

If he was trying for an effect, he had succeeded. He must have been six foot four, though his height was accentuated by the thinness of his frame. Not that he was puny. His arms and legs seemed to have a wiry sort of strength to the. Longish black hair was swept back from a peak on his forehead and there was just a touch of grey at his temples. He might have been thirty, he might have been a fit fifty for that matter. He was dressed in tight black pants and a black shirt that was buttoned up around his neck. All that was missing was a cape, and I got the impression that one was probably hanging on a coat rack in the back room. I fought back an urge to look at his teeth to see if his incisors were pointy.

"Is there anything in particular that you are interested in?" he asked pronouncing particular as three distinct words, "par tic ular." His vowels had an odd shape to them, but I was hard pressed whether to place them as from some middle European country or a B horror movie.

"Not really. I'm just satisfying my curiosity."

"Curiosity can be a dangerous thing." It was posed as a statement rather than a threat, but I was getting the idea.

"Without curiosity, how does one learn anything? I gathered from the sign out front that you were in the business of spreading wisdom."

"True. But only to the true believers or those who come with an empty mind and a willingness to accept."

"I've been accused of having an empty mind. I'm not sure about the willingness to accept part, Mr.—"

"Romanescu, Vladimir Romanescu. I am the Master of this house." As with the girl, the way he said Master made it obvious it was capitalized. "And you are?"

"Me? I'm just a nobody."

"We are what we choose to be."

"I'll have to remember that. Is that one of your bits of esoteric wisdom?"

"Take it as you like."

I've dealt with my share of con men over the years. Romanescu reminded me of them, but there was something more sinister lurking behind the patter.

"Natasha said that you mentioned a name?"

"Yes. Anna Smerchek. She was a student at the university. I thought you might know her."

"Anna Smerchek? No, the name is unfamiliar to me. But then many of the students wander through here out of, as you said, curiosity." I couldn't tell if he was lying or not. I have to admit, he was charming, though, in his own creepy way.

"I was told by a friend of hers that she had been here. But as you say, lots of students wander through." I waved a hand at the empty room.

"Just what is your interest, Mr.—?"

"No one has seen Anna for a few months. Since late October, in fact. I was kind of hoping maybe you or your assistant might shed some light on that."

"Are you with the police? You have that sort of aura about you."

"No, I'm not with the police. I've been hired by Anna's family to look into her disappearance. I'm a private investigator. I can show you my license if you like."

"That won't be necessary. Your aura is enough for me to believe you. You say this Anna came here?"

"To one of your lectures or sermons or whatever they are."

"I prefer to think of them as just talks. I find it less formal."

"I have a picture of her if you'd care to take a look." I pulled out the photo her parents had given me and showed it to him.

"A lovely, girl. But no, I do not remember her," he said shaking his head with a trace of sadness. I wondered if it was because he hadn't met her, or because he had knowledge of her fate.

"The boy she was with said you spoke to her after the lecture."

"I try to greet each of the attendees to my talks. To gage their interest so see if it is genuine or just casual curiosity. But I only remember them if they return, I'm afraid."

"Well, I won't take up more of your time, Mr. Romanescu, but here is my card if you should remember anything." I handed him one of my business cards and as an afterthought passed one to the shop girl who took it with disinterest.

As I let myself out I thought I could feel the gaze of Romanescu drilling into my back. My knee almost gave out on the porch steps in my haste to be out of there and I had to catch my breath once I had made it to the sidewalk.

There was no doubt that Romanescu was putting on an act. No one could be that creepy without it being intentional. The whole polite façade over the sinister backdrop had been carefully constructed. The question was why? Was it just a marketing ploy, something to lure in the marks, or was there something more behind it? One thing I was sure of, he knew more about Anna Smerchek than he was letting on.

9.

After I got back to the office, I decided to give Murphy a call. I didn't really know if there was any connection between Romanescu and Anna, but I was pretty sure that The House of Esoteric Wisdom was a cover for something.

"Homicide, Sgt. Murphy speaking."

When I told him who it was, he didn't seem that happy to hear from me.

"Are you still trying to fleece money from that poor girl's family?"

"You don't have to worry, Murphy. At this point, I'm only charging the original retainer and expenses, which so far haven't been much. Anyone else would be bleeding them dry. At least I'm making an honest effort."

"Oh? So have you found out anything that us professionals missed?"

"I don't know. Maybe. Did the name Vladimir Romanescu ever come up in connection to the case?"

"Vladimir Romanescu? Are you kidding? Did you make that name up?"

"No. It's a real guy, though that might not be his real name."

"Never heard of him," Murphy said, sounding tired.

"How about The House of Esoteric Wisdom?"

"Never heard of that, either. What's the link with the Smercheck girl?"

"I'm not sure. I ran into a wanna-be boyfriend of Anna's through Professor Hazeltine. He said that he took her to this place called The House of Esoteric Wisdom for a lecture by the guy who runs the place, Romanescu. This was about the time that her roommate said Anna's personality started to change, about the end of September."

"Nothing like that ever came up in the investigation."

"The kid, the boyfriend, didn't want to get involved. He seemed a nice enough kid, but I think he was worried that his parents would be mad if he was linked to a murder investigation."

"Disappearance," Murphy corrected, but we both had our doubts. "So why'd this kid open up to you?"

"I think he was feeling guilty that he might have be in some way responsible for whatever happened to Anna."

"OK. So what's this House of External Wisdom or whatever it's called?"

"The House of Esoteric Wisdom. On the surface it seems to be some kind of occult bookstore. They sell books on astrology, magic, fortune telling, that kind of thing. Also black candles, occult jewelry, stuff like that. It's in an old house in the student section. I get the impression that this Romanescu gives lectures, he calls them 'talks,' to drum up business. On the surface, it looked as legitimate as that sort of place can get."

"But—?"

"I don't see how a place like that could pull in enough money to even cover the rent, let alone salaries and a profit. It's got to be a front for something."

The phone went silent for a moment. I could visualize Murphy putting two and two together on the other end. "That something being drugs? Is that what you're thinking? I never turned up any evidence that the Smercheck girl was into any kind of drugs. Not even alcohol."

"Maybe that was the problem?"

"Are you thinking that she might have seen something and that was the cause of her disappearance?"

"It's a theory. I didn't see any signs of drugs when I checked the place out, but they wouldn't keep that stuff out in the open. All I know is the place didn't add up to me. It has to be some kind of front."

"So what's this Romanescu like? What kind of name is Romanescu, anyhow?"

"I think it's Romanian, or maybe Transylvanian." I answered.

"You're making this up again, aren't you? What's he really like?"

"Seen any old vampire movies lately? The ones with Bela Lugosi? Well this Romanescu guy looks and talks like a younger Lugosi. Dresses all in black, talks with this heavy middle European sort of accent. Really creepy, but suave and sophisticated at the same time. I don't know if it's real, or he's just putting on an act, but if it's an act, he's one hell of an actor."

"Next you're going to tell me that he sports a set of fangs?"

"I didn't get a good look at the inside of his mouth. But it wouldn't surprise me."

"I really don't need this shit."

"Look, don't blame me. I'm just reporting what I've found out like a good citizen."

"Yeah, yeah. Look, this is a completely new angle to me. Let me check with Narcotics and see if they've got anything on Romanescu or this Wisdom place. Maybe Bunko, too. Fortune tellers are their line. I'll get back to you if anything turns up."

"Sure." I got the feeling I was getting the brush off.

"No, I mean it. And thanks for the tip."

I really wasn't expecting to hear back from Murphy. I couldn't blame him. I had to admit it was a pretty strange story. I spent the rest of the afternoon worrying about what I was going to tell Anna's parents. I didn't care about the money, I never really had, but somehow I had hoped that I'd be able to give them some closure, some certainty about what had happened to their daughter. It wasn't looking good in that department.

I was surprised when Murphy called me back just before six. He said he didn't want to talk over the phone, but could I meet him at The Dead End around seven.

Murphy was nursing a beer at the bar when I got there. When he saw me come in he nodded toward a table in the back and then got the bartender to pour a couple of more.

"So, what's up?" I asked after a first sip of beer.

"I asked around like I said I would."

"And—"

"Narcotics is aware of the place. They've got a file on it. Like you said, it would be the perfect cover for distributing drugs. Kids wandering in and out at all hours, coming out with packages, shipments arriving disguised as books, what more could you ask for. The only problem is that Narcotics never could find any drugs. They sent in guys undercover, even got some students to try and buy stuff. No luck. This Romanescu guy seemed downright hostile to the suggestion of selling drugs. He even reported one of the undercover cops to the police. If there are drugs moving through the place, they aren't being sold over the counter."

"So it's not drugs. Something else has got you worked up."

"Let me tell it my own way, will you?" Murphy protested. "I checked with Bunko, too. They'd checked it out. No dice. The girl that works the counter will read Tarot cards if you ask, but she won't take money. She just does it as a 'demonstration.' Anyway, according to the guy from Bunko the profile is all wrong. The kind of people that go in there, kids and college students don't usually have enough money to make any of the normal scams worth running. They've given it a pass."

"What aren't you telling me?"

"OK. This is where it get's interesting. But this is all hush-hush. You can't let any of this get out. You've got to give me your word."

"You've got it."

"I talked to the Juvenile department. They've had their eye on the place, too."

"What for?"

"It turns out that this House of Wisdom has got kind of a reputation on the runaway's circuit. Seems they're always ready to supply a free meal or provide a place to crash for the night. This Romanescu character acts like he's an easy touch for any kid who's all alone and needs help. Food, a bed, money."

"What aren't you saying? Is Romanescu abusing these kids? Is he a recruiter for human trafficking? Something like that?"

"Well, that's what Juvey thought, except there's no evidence of that. They'll give any underage kid a free meal, or a bed for the night, but then they refer them to social services or one of the church groups that handle those sort of things. No pressure, just a suggestion, but no second night or second meal. Not if you're underage."

"I sense a big but coming."

"Well, it seems this Romanescu has a thing for young girls, just not too young. Not under age. He's real careful that way. But he's been creating a sort of cult following composed of mostly girls, though there do seem to be a few young men, too. But all over eighteen. Juvenile Justice can't do anything because they're all of age, and none of the ones involved have ever come forward with any sort of complaint. Most of the recruits seem to be loners, anyway. Former runaways, kids that got kicked out by their parents when they turned eighteen, that sort of thing. Juvenile keeps tabs on the place, but hasn't found anything to act on."

"So what happens to these kids?"

"That's the strange part. No one knows. A couple of them seem to work at the bookstore or in the house cooking and cleaning, but most of them just seem to come, hang out for awhile and then disappear."

"And you think that's what happened to Anna Smerchek?"

"There's no evidence that she got caught up in this cult. Until you found out that she'd gone to a lecture there, there was nothing to link her to Romanescu or the House of Wisdom. Besides, she doesn't fit the profile. She had family, she was a student, she had people who knew her."

"But it does seem that she fell under some sort of influence in the weeks before she disappeared."

"Yeah. But whose? One could just as easily make a case for the professor, what's his name, Hazeltine."

"Hazeltine seems alright to me," I said, for some reason defending him.

"Yeah, I'm just saying there's no evidence. What can we do? There's no way I could go before a judge and get a warrant to search the place. And, in case you haven't noticed, people have gotten real sensitive about 'police harassment' lately."

"So you're just going to drop it?"

"I didn't say that. We'll keep an eye on Romanescu, but until some sort of real evidence turns up, there's not much else we can do. You were a cop long enough to understand that."

The problem was I did understand exactly what Murphy was telling me. Without evidence linking Anna to Romanescu, even investigating might be considered grounds for a law suit.

"Is there at least something that I can tell Anna's parents?"

Murphy stared into his beer for a moment. "You can tell them that the police are investigating some new leads but they aren't divulging details at the moment. Just don't tell them any of what I've told you. You understand?"

"Yeah. I understand. Do you want another beer?"

"No, I better get going."

Murphy got up and left. Me, I had another beer, and then one more.

10.

I decided to call the Smercheks the next day. I'd given the case my best effort. Maybe I'd even turned up a fresh lead for the police to work on. Other than that, I was pretty much at a dead end. I'd could continue to poke around, but I'd be wasting my time and the Smerchek's money.

"Smerchek's Hardware," the voice on the phone answered in an up north accent. "Vern speaking."

We exchanged pleasantries for about fifteen seconds then I got to the heart of things.

"You've found out something about Anna?" Vern asked in, with both hope and fear in his voice.

"No, not really. I've looked into the case like we agreed. I'm afraid that I haven't turned up any new clues. I've talked to the police detective on the case as well, Sergeant Murphy. I know him from when I was on the force, and he's a good man. The police are still working the case and they haven't given up hope."

"That's what they said months ago. I know how things work. They say the case is open, but the detective on it has other cases, too, and only so much time, so unless something drops in their lap, they aren't going to do anything."

"I don't think that's quite fair, Mr. Smerchek—"

"Not knowing what happened to Anna isn't fair. It's eating my wife up alive."

"I understand that—"

"Do you? Do you have a daughter? A son?"

"No, I don't—"

"Then you don't understand."

The phone was silent except for the breathing on the other end. Vern Smerchek had worked himself up and he was taking it out on me. I can't say that I blamed him. This was probably the first time he'd really let himself go. There was nothing I could say that would change things, so I just waited. Finally after nearly a minute he apologized:

"I'm sorry. I shouldn't take it out on you. Or your policeman friend. Is there anything more that you can do?"

"I don't think so. I've interviewed everybody who knew her at the university. Her roommate, her professors, even a boy she went to a movie with. None of them had any idea of what might have happened to Anna. I've pretty much reached the same dead end as the police did."

"Do you need more money? Is that it?" Smerchek was working himself up again.

"No, it's not a matter of money, Mr. Smerchek. Believe me, if I thought it would do any good, I'd be happy to take your money to investigate further. But right now the way things are it would just be a waste of your money. As it is, I feel bad that I don't have more to tell you for what you've paid me already."

"I'm sure," Smerchek said, a trace of sarcasm tingeing his small-town businessman's voice.

"Don't misunderstand me, Mr. Smerchek. I spent nearly three full days on the case, maybe more than that, and I'd have been happy to charge you my full rates if I'd turned up anything. But the fact is, despite my best efforts, I didn't. I'm willing to take the two-fifty you paid me and call us square. I'll include an account of time spent along with my written report if you want."

"I'm sorry. I didn't mean to imply you were cheating me. I'm just so frustrated by the whole thing. And worried."

"I appreciate that, Mr. Smerchek. I'll tell you what I'll do. I'll keep my eyes and ears open, and if I hear of anything that I think is worth following up on, I'll let you know and we can take it from there. How's that?"

"Sure. That sounds fine. Thank you for calling. I've got a customer in the store and I've got to go. Good-bye," and the line went dead.

After that, I tried to forget about Anna Smerchek. I'd done what I could for her family, but as far as I'd been able to discover, Anna had disappeared without leaving a trace. Murphy had looked into Romanescu and the House of Esoteric Wisdom, but that had proved to be a dead end. There was no physical evidence linking Anna to either of them, and Romanescu and his followers had disavowed ever having seen her.

March turned into April, the snow finally melted, the first blushes of green appeared. And there things stood—until they found Anna's body.

11.

I got the call from Murphy in my office. It was still before noon. All he said was, "She's been found." He sounded a little shaky.

I didn't have to ask who he meant, but I did anyway. "Anna?"

"Yes. Look, I can't explain it over the phone. You'd better come down here and see for yourself." I scrambled for a pencil to write down the address that came over the phone.

"I'll be there as soon as I can."

"I'll be here," he said grimly and then hung up.

Murphy was a veteran of the Homicide Squad. I knew he'd been in Vietnam, too, though he never talked about it. It made me wonder what could have affected him so to produce that reaction in him.

The address he'd given me was in a neighborhood not far from campus, another block of turn of the century frame houses, mostly two stories, mostly converted to house students. As I looked for a parking place, I realized that I was only a few blocks from the House of Esoteric Wisdom.

The street had been blocked off by a pair of squad cars with their red lights flashing, and the crime scene van and a truck from the Medical Examiner's office were parked out front. One of the TV stations had a truck there as well, but the patrolmen were keeping them at a distance.

At some point there'd been a fire in the house up in the attic or the second floor. A blue tarp covered a hole that had been burned in the roof and black soot stained the white siding around the second floor windows. It had happened some time ago, long enough for the first floor windows to have been boarded up and for several layers of graffiti to have covered over the plywood.

The patrolmen at the barricades weren't going to let me through, either, until I showed my license, then the uniform sergeant who was in charge gave the okay to let me through.

"Murphy said to expect you. Go around in back." The sergeant who was in his fifties and near retirement looked a little pale around the edges.

I walked down the narrow driveway that ran between the burnt out house and the one next door. Someone had thrown up on the few daffodils that grew in the thin strip of soil next to the foundation. My own gut tightened as I imagined what I was going to find.

There was another cop standing guard in front of a bulkhead door that led into the cellar. He looked up as I rounded the corner, but he must have figured that if I'd gotten that far I was okay. I could hear Murphy's voice coming up from the cellar where he was quietly talking to someone, but I couldn't pick up the words. The cop just nodded towards the steps leading downward.

The steps going down were narrow and made of cement. Going down stairs is always hardest on my leg. I took them slowly, moving my right leg first on each step. The cellar was about what you'd expect in a house like that, low ceilinged, damp, and dirty with low beams and plumbing hanging underneath. The naked light bulbs had been augmented by some lights that the crime scene team had brought in.

Murphy was standing near the doorway talking to a man that I took to be from the M.E.'s office.

"She's in there." He indicated a doorway into another room towards the front of the house. "You can go and look. Just don't touch anything."

I went on through. It was cold and damp. I realized the furnace had probably been turned off since the fire. A rivulet of dirty water ran down the center of the floor to a drain.

There were a couple of guys from the crime scene team taking pictures, the flashes of their cameras going off every few seconds blinding me. That was why I didn't see the body at first. Sensing my presence, the photographers backed off to let me through. I think they were just glad to get out of there.

It wasn't a large room, maybe ten by twelve. One wall of it was the space that must have been a coal bunker before the furnace was switched to oil. The other two were the cement blocks of the front right corner of the house. A small window with dirty panes of glass was set high in the wall on the side of the house. In the middle of the room was a big table. It looked like it might have been a kitchen table at one time. Anna's body was lying on top of it.

At first I thought she looked peaceful. She was laid out on her back, legs extended, her arms folded across her breast. Her hair had been arranged neatly under her head. She was wearing a long white dress. It wasn't a normal dress, not even a wedding dress. There was something ceremonial about it, almost liturgical in nature, as if she had dressed for some ritual.

I moved in to get a closer look at the face. It was Anna, alright. There was no doubt about that. But I realized that her death hadn't been peaceful. Underneath the wide sleeves of the dress I could see the marks where her hands had been bound. A glance at her ankles showed that those had been tied as well, though there were no signs of the cords that had dug into her flesh.

Looking back at her face, I saw that her skin seemed unnaturally white. There were no signs of decomposition. It occurred to me that with the furnace turned off, the cellar had probably been below freezing until the last few weeks. Even then it would have been as cold as an icebox.

Her eyes were still open, staring blindly at the ceiling. I had an urge to close them, as if it would finally give Anna a chance to rest, but when my fingers went to the cold flesh of her lids I found they wouldn't move. I took one last look at the face, letting the image burn into my memory, and then turned back to Murphy.

"What do you know?" I asked.

"Her body was found this morning by a building inspector. He was checking the place over because a demolition permit had been requested. He was pretty shaken up over it, but he called in as soon as he felt up to it."

"What about the fire?"

"The fire happened months ago. Early November. Between the fire and the fire department the roof was pretty much gutted. The house was abandoned and the owner has been waiting on the insurance to tear it down."

"So Anna was placed here sometime after the fire?"

"Yeah. Hard to say when. The adjuster from the insurance company made his examination about a week after the fire. No one has been in the building since, until today. Not much doubt about the cause of the fire. It was a cooking fire in the upstairs apartment."

"Any idea when Anna died?" I hoped for my sake that it was sometime before the day the Smercheks came to my office.

"Are you kidding?" the man who Murphy had been talking to said.

"This is Dr. Morton from the M.E.'s office," Murphy explained. "Doc, this is a private investigator hired by the girl's parents."

"It's impossible to say at this point," Morton said apologetically. "It was some time ago. Probably months. I don't know if I'll be able to say anything more definitive after the autopsy, but judging from the condition of the body, I'd say that it's been frozen and only thawed recently. More than that, you're guess is as good as mine. It could have been anytime from late November to early March."

"Any idea about the cause of death? I know you've probably told the Sergeant all this, but I'll be reporting to the parents."

"I'll know more after the autopsy. We'll have to test for drugs, of course. There are no obvious signs of trauma, no blows to the head, no broken bones or wounds. Well, no wounds except for two small punctures to the side of the neck."

"Punctures?" I asked.

"Yes, almost like bite marks, except there are no marks of any other teeth. It's possible that they were made post-mortem, after death. There's one other thing. It appears that the body has been exsanguinated."

"Excuse me?"

"Sorry. The body has been drained of blood. Presumably shortly after death, but I can't be sure without an autopsy. That's the cause of the extreme pallor of the skin."

"Are you saying that someone tied Anna up and drained the blood from her body."

"That's for you gentlemen to determine. I can only comment on the state of the body. Is it alright for my men to remove the body now, Sergeant?"

"Might as well go ahead, doc. I think the crime scene boys have taken all the pictures they can stomach. Please let me know what you find as soon as possible."

"Of course." The doctor turned and went up the stairs.

I looked at Murphy. "You do know what this looks like, don't you?"

"What do you think it looks like?" Murphy responded slowly.

"It looks like Anna was attacked by a vampire. Or at least someone who thinks he's a vampire."

"I know. That's why I want you to keep a lid on it. I only let you down here because you were working for the girl's parents, and they deserve to know. But if word of the details get out to the press, who knows what might happen."

"Don't worry, Murphy. I won't say anything to the papers. You'll let me know what the M.E. reports?"

"Yeah."

"I'll tell the parents, if you want."

"That might be best. Somebody from the department will have to make the official call, but that could take a couple of days. That will give you time."

"Thanks. Any ideas on who could be responsible?"

"I don't believe in vampires. Do you?"

"No. But some psycho who thinks he's one? Maybe."

"What about your professor friend?"

"Hazeltine? You're joking, aren't you?"

"Why? It seems to me he's mighty interested in vampires."

"And werewolves and old movies and all sorts of strange things. But that doesn't mean he deluded himself into thinking he's any of those."

"You're probably right," Murphy said with a shrug. "This case has got me wound up. Especially after today. It's out of my range of experience."

"Mine, too."

I left it at that. The M.E.'s crew was coming down the stairs, so I got out of their way and left.

12.

Telling Anna's parents wasn't something you could do over the phone. At least I couldn't. I owed them that much. I couldn't tell you why I felt that way, but I did. Somewhere along the line this case had become personal for me.

Besides, it was a great day for a drive. The sun was shining, the sky was blue, the snow had melted for the most part, and there were hints of green in the fields. Any other day and it would have been a pleasant drive in the country.

The drive took me an hour and a half, mostly on two lane state roads heading straight north. It wasn't a long drive, really, mostly at sixty five, slowing only occasionally for a one street town that consisted of a gas station, a couple of bars on opposite sides of the street with the odd feed store or farm implement dealership tossed in for color. And a church. There always was a church, two if the area was divided between Lutherans and Catholics. Small towns tend to take their religion more seriously than we do in the city.

The town Anna was from was a little larger, maybe five thousand people or so, but I still didn't have much trouble finding the hardware store. It was located about where you'd imagine, in the middle of a block on Main St. It looked about like you'd expect, too, an older building with a tall false front over two large plate glass windows flanking the door. An array of gardening implements were displayed in one of the windows along with a big sign proclaiming "Spring Sale." The other window held a lawn mower and some snow shovels with another sign declaring "end of season sale" over them. Some flats of marigolds and other flowers had been arranged on stands in front on the sidewalk. There was plenty of parking in front.

Stepping through the front door was like walking back in time. There was a little bell over the front door that tinkled as it opened. The floor was made up of wooden strips that showed the wear of eighty years in its undulations. Shelves of plumbing fixtures, nuts and bolts, and electrical fixtures lined one wall. The other was mostly taken up with racks of tools, ladders, shovels and all the other things in that line you might need. The middle of the store was given over to tables carrying the more domestic goods, one for canning jars, another for small appliances like toasters and roasters.

In the back wall was a kind of office behind a counter with an old cash register. That's where Vern was, talking on the phone with a customer. He didn't see me at first, or if he did, he must of thought I was just another customer coming in for some carrot seeds or eight penny nails. When he recognized me, his phone conversation hesitated in mid sentence. He picked it up after a second, promised to get whatever they had wanted and hung up.

"Anna's been found, hasn't she?" he asked. His voice was even, but the emotions were apparent. I was glad there was no one else in the store.

"Yes. This morning."

"She's dead, isn't she?"

"Yes. I'm sorry." There didn't seem much else to respond with.

"How?"

"It's not completely clear at the moment. The cause of death will have to wait on the autopsy. There wasn't any obvious signs of trauma." No signs, that is, except for the fact she'd been drained of blood.

"Do they know when she died?" I was surprised at how well Vern was taking it, asking his relevant questions in an organized way. It might have been better if he'd broken down and cried.

"Again, they're not sure. It seems likely that it was some time ago. She was found in the cellar of a house close to the campus. There'd been a fire there in early November and it had been sitting abandoned. She could have been put there any time after the fire."

"You say put there. Does that mean she was murdered?"

"Probably. Again, that will have to wait on the medical examiner, but it seems likely."

Vern Smerchek put his hands to his face. It was the first sign of emotion that he had revealed, but I could tell that he was poised on the edge.

Finally he asked, "Had she been—you know—?"

"Had she been sexually assaulted?" I answered, avoiding the more explicit term. "I don't think so."

"I need to know so I can prepare Ellen if I have to. If she'd been raped." There it was, out in the open.

"There were no signs of anything like that where she was found. She was fully clothed." I didn't add that she had been posed in what appeared to be a kind of ritual gown. "As I said, there were no obvious signs of violence."

"You saw her?"

"Yeah. The cops called me when they found the body. Sgt. Murphy knew I was working for you. Like I said, she was found in the cellar of an abandoned house. There wasn't any heat on in the place, so the body froze. It was just starting to thaw when she was found by a workman, so there wasn't really any decomposition."

Smerchek looked at me. He was a mild man with small town good manners, but there was a sudden hardness behind his eyes.

"There's something you're not telling me. What is it?"

"It appears, and the police are still collecting evidence, that Anna was not murdered where she was found. Someone brought the body to that house after she was dead and—well they didn't just dump her. She was laid out very carefully on a table in the cellar."

"What do you mean 'laid out'?"

"She was posed. Almost as if it were some kind of religious ritual of some sort."

Smerchek had been poised between grief and anger. The anger finally got the better of him. "What do you mean posed?"

I explained what I'd seen in the cellar

"What kind of person does that to a young girl? Poses a corpse? Leaves her body to freeze in a burnt out house? What kind of a monster?"

"I don't know, Mr. Smerchek. Both the police and I want to find out. We will find out. I promise you."

And suddenly as it had come, the anger was gone.

"I'm sorry for the way I acted on the phone the other day. You were just doing your job. You were just being honest."

"That's okay, Mr. Smerchek. I understood."

"You didn't have to come all this way to tell me in person. I appreciate that."

"It was the least I could do."

"It was more than a lot of men would have done. From what you say, Anna had been dead a long time before we contacted you. There wasn't anything you could have done to change that."

"That's probably true, Mr. Smerchek. It doesn't make it any better from my standpoint."

"No. I can see that."

An awkward silence followed. There didn't seem to be anything to say.

"The police will be calling you in a day or so. You'll have to go down and make a formal identification."

"They are sure it's Anna, aren't they?"

"Yes, but they like to have a close relative identify the body in these cases. It's procedure."

"Of course," Smerchek said, shaking his head.

"Would you like me to speak to your wife?"

"No. That won't be necessary. It will be better if I tell her myself. But thank you for the offer."

"Is there anything else I can do for you, Mr. Smerchek?"

"No. You've done what we asked. You found Anna."

"If there's nothing else then, I'll be going."

"Yes, thank you for coming," he said, then added, "You will get him, won't you? The one responsible?"

"It's a police matter now, Mr. Smerchek. An active investigation. But it's a murder case. They take those very seriously. They'll find the one responsible."

"Yes. I hope they do."

The sun was going down as I drove home, casting long shadows as I headed south. After a half hour I stopped in one of the little towns to have a burger and a shot and a beer. I felt like having another, but I knew if I did, I might not stop, so after I finished the burger, I paid my bill and drove the rest of the way home.

HAZELTINE

13.

It was several days after I returned from my trip up north. I was sitting in my office trying to forget Anna Smerchek when the phone rang. I answered to an angry voice practically shouting:

"What did you tell the them?"

I'd never heard him use that tone of voice, but I knew that it was Professor Hazeltine.

"Tell who, professor?"

"The police, that's who," he replied belligerently.

"I haven't told them anything. What's this all about?"

"You must have said something to them. That detective, Murphy, has been running around asking questions about me. He's even subpoenaed my personnel files from the university. He seems to have gotten it into his mind that I had something to do with Anna Smerchek's death."

"Look, professor," I said, trying to placate him, "I haven't told Murphy anything to implicate you. I fact I've told him several times that I didn't think you had anything to do with her murder."

"Murder! Anna was murdered?"

The police hadn't released any details of Anna's death yet, only the fact that her body had been discovered and that the circumstances were being investigated.

"I shouldn't be telling you this, professor, but Anna was definitely murdered. Probably sometime in November. She was killed and then her body was stashed in the cellar of a burnt out house."

"That's terrible," Hazeltine said, regaining some of his composure. "But why would they think that I was involved?"

I weighed how much I should tell Hazeltine. I didn't think that he was involved, but that was just my personal feeling. There was always a chance that Murphy was right. I decided to go with my gut.

"It's like this, professor. There were certain aspects of the way that Anna's body was found that indicate—well—there was something ceremonial about the way the body had been posed after it was taken to the cellar."

"Okay. It's my understanding that it's not unusual for serial killers to engage in ritualistic behavior. It's not my field, of course, but I've read a bit. I still don't understand why Murphy thinks it has something to do with me."

"Like I said, there were some aspects of the crime scene that were pretty unusual."

"And—"

"OK. To be blunt about it, Anna's body was laid out on a table in a long white dress. All of the blood had been drained from her body."

"I still don't understand," Hazeltine complained.

"There were two small puncture wounds to her neck. They looked like bite marks."

"Bite marks?" Then it dawned on the professor what I had been skirting. "My God! Are you saying this thick headed detective thinks that Anna's death was the work of a vampire? And because I've written about the subject he considers me a suspect? Does he think I'm an actual vampire?"

"It looks that way, professor. Murphy didn't talk to me about it, but if he's investigating you, that must be what he's thinking."

"But that's ridiculous," Hazeltine sputtered. "Vampires are a myth, a fantasy. They aren't real. And I certainly am not a vampire. I walk in the daylight! I like garlic!"

"I don't think Murphy believes the killer is a real vampire, professor. He just thinks that the killer thinks he's a vampire."

"So? What you're saying is that he thinks I'm a nut job that goes around draining the blood out of coeds. I know some of my colleagues think I'm a bit eccentric, but the only reason I'm interested in vampires and werewolves and all those kind of things is because I find them amusing and interesting. No, what I really mean to say is that I find what other people think about those kind of things interesting, that and the way they've been portrayed in literature and movies provide insight into the human mind. I no more believe myself a vampire than you do. The whole idea is absurd."

"I agree with you, professor. But the fact is that it appears someone thinks he's a vampire, or at least is acting that way. And he has killed at least once. And the victim was a former student of yours."

"So are hundreds of other people."

"But they didn't end up on a slab in a nightdress with bite marks on their necks and all of their blood gone."

"Now you're starting to sound like you're taking this detective's viewpoint seriously."

"Relax, professor. I still don't think you were involved in any way. But I know how cops think and I can understand why Murphy is investigating you. I'd probably be doing the same if I was in his position."

"Well, you've got to talk him out of it."

"I don't know if I can, professor. Murphy can be pretty stubborn. Like a bulldog. And I don't have any official standing in the case. Especially since Anna has been found. That's what her parents hired me for, and that's done now."

"You don't understand. This could ruin me. Universities hate scandal of any kind. For a professor to be accused of murder is about the worst kind of scandal imaginable. As it is, there are some people in the department that aren't too thrilled with me. They resent my popularity with the students and they are against anything that smacks of popular culture. Literature isn't like the sciences. We don't get big research grants from the government. There's a lot of jealousy over the fact that my books actually sell and that I made money consulting on a film. Talk about being after blood, there are a couple faculty members who'd love to see mine."

"Don't get excited, professor. Murphy is just poking around. It's what he gets paid to do. It will take a lot more evidence than your interest in vampires to get the D.A. to issue an arrest warrant."

"It doesn't matter if I'm arrested or not. Well of course it does, but even if I'm not arrested, the mere fact that I was under suspicion could taint my reputation and end my career. I can't believe this is happening. It's like something out of Kafka."

"The best thing then, is to hope that Murphy finds the real killer, and quickly."

"Well, he doesn't seem to be looking in the right places. Not if he's concentrating on me."

"Then maybe we have to help him along."

"What do you mean?"

"Whoever killed Anna seems to be acting out some kind of vampire fantasy. From what I know, you're probably the biggest expert on the subject around. At least in this town. Maybe if you could give me some insights into what the killer is thinking, what fantasy he's tuned in to, I might be able to point Murphy in the right direction."

"That almost sounds sensible. What do you want to know?"

"Not over the phone. Why don't we meet someplace to talk it over?"

"OK. You're office? I don't think it would be wise to meet at mine."

"No. It might not look to good if Murphy tracked you here. Someplace neutral. Someplace where we might just accidentally run into each other."

"I understand. You don't want to risk the taint of associating with a known vampire. How about Sid's?"

Sid's was a sort of cocktail bar not far from the campus. It was quiet, and a little too upscale to have become a student hangout.

"That sounds good. About seven?"

The professor agreed and hung up.

I sat there thinking. Murphy might be stubborn at times, but he was usually pretty level-headed. Was there something that he knew about the professor that I didn't? I really didn't know the little guy all that well and my experiences with intellectual types was pretty limited. Could he have fooled me that completely?

14.

Hazeltine was waiting for me when I arrived at Sid's. From the empty glass sitting on the bar in front of him, it looked like he'd been there awhile. I took the spot next to him, caught the bartender's eye and ordered rye on the rocks. The professor ordered another gin and tonic.

After the drinks came we moved to one of the booths opposite the bar where we could talk in private.

"You look worried, Professor." It was true. Hazeltine had that hunted look, the kind men get when they feel things closing in on them.

"I've got every right to be worried. I think Murphy is having someone follow me."

"That doesn't happen much in real life, Professor," I explained. "It takes too much manpower to do it correctly. A stakeout, maybe, because that only takes two men working in shifts, but even then, it usually only done when there's a high probability that a crime is going to go down where they can catch someone in the act. Why do you think you're being followed?"

"I've got this feeling. Like eyes burning holes in my back."

"It's probably just your imagination. Have you actually spotted someone?"

"No. Not for sure. I don't know. This whole thing has got me upset. Do you have any idea what it's like being suspected of a horrible crime like this?"

"Not really, Professor," I admitted. "Anyway, if you didn't do it, and you have no plans to commit a major crime it might not be such a bad thing if the police were tailing you. You'd have a witness as to where you were."

"That's very reassuring." He pulled out a pack of cigarettes, thought better of it and shoved it back into his jacket pocket.

"Look, we didn't come here to discuss whether you're being tailed or not, Professor. The best way to get the police off your back is to find out who killed Anna Smerchek, but to do that I need to figure out what kind of man I'm dealing with."

"Are you still involved in the case? I thought Anna's parents hired you to find her. Well, you've done that, or at least the police have. And quit calling me Professor. You're not one of my students. My name is George."

"Sure thing—George. I'm not working for the Smerchek's anymore. Or at least I'm not taking their money. But I figure I owe them something."

"It sounds like you're taking Anna's death personally."

"You didn't have to tell her father that her daughter had been laid out on a table and drained of her blood. I did." I took a long pull on my rye.

"I didn't know. I'm sorry. It must have been rough. I thought the police handled things like that."

"I felt I owed it to the Smercheks. They'd paid me to find their daughter—alive. I failed."

"But you said the police thought that she was probably killed in November. That was months before the Smercheks came to you."

"It doesn't really matter, does it?"

"No, I guess not." He reached inside his jacket for the pack of cigarettes, but stopped half way. "What did you want to talk to me about, anyhow?"

"I'm trying to get some idea, you'd probably call it an insight, into what was going on in the killer's head when he killed Anna. Like I said earlier, there are aspects of how the body was found that suggests he really thinks he's a vampire or at least he's acting that way. You're the only person I know who knows anything about vampires."

"What I know about vampires is how they've been portrayed in books and movies. I can tell you just about every movie that's ever been made featuring vampires, about Bram Stoker's play, even about classical references to them. But that's all fiction. As far as I know vampires aren't real."

"That's just the point—George," I was going to say "Professor" but stopped myself at the last minute. "If we accept the fact that whoever killed Anna wasn't really a vampire, then whatever it is they imagine they are came from watching those movies and reading those books. That's the kind of thing that I want to get a handle on."

"That makes sense. Why don't you start by describing the scene where they found Anna?"

"I don't know if I should," I protested. "It's an open case and the police aren't giving out details."

"How can I tell you what the killer is thinking if I don't have anything to work with? If you describe the scene, I might be able to tell you what movie or book it came from. In my position I certainly am not going to blab details to the papers or TV. Either you trust me or you don't."

"You're right." I took another slug of rye and then began to describe the scene in the cellar. Hazeltine kept asking questions, going for more details. That just made it worse, but I told him all I could remember.

"Well, to start off, some of what you've described is fairly generic to vampire tales. For example, the long white dress. That's used in all sorts of sacred rituals. Take christenings or confirmations. But the usage also goes back to some of the earliest vampire films where the 'brides of Dracula' were dressed in white with long unbound hair. The cellar is another generic point, a reference to crypts. One of the persistent images in vampire lore is the coffin hidden in a crypt or cellar containing soil from the vampire's native country that is used by the vampire to rest in during the day."

"Great. All that tells us is that this guy watched a bunch of old Dracula movies when he was a kid. Didn't everyone?"

"Granted. But there are other aspects of the scene that are perhaps more specific. First of all, Anna's body was laid out on a table. That's a very ritualistic kind of thing to do, almost as if the table was an altar. Yet, from what you've said, she wasn't killed in that cellar and her blood was drained someplace else as well."

"Yeah, that's what forensics said. What difference does it make? I guess I'm not following you."

"One question that we have to ask is whether Anna was a victim or an acolyte?"

"What do you mean?"

"Was she killed just as a source of blood to fill some psychotic craving for nourishment on the part of the killer, or was her death an attempt to turn her into another vampire? If she had been killed just to provide food, the body could have been disposed of anywhere. The only reason to hide the body in that case would be to avoid detection. But Anna was laid out in a very formal way, not so much concealed as sheltered. It's almost as if the killer expected her to come back to life, not as a mortal, but as another vampire. The cellar where her body was placed was chosen very carefully, an abandoned house where sunlight couldn't reach her body, placed on an altar where her corpse could rest until reanimation."

"That's creepy."

"Of course it is. That's part of the appeal of the vampire legends. The horror lies in the fact that it's almost a parody of the Christian belief in an afterlife."

"So are you trying to say that Anna participated in this ritual willingly? That she wanted to become a vampire?"

"Anna was a very impressionable young woman, but I don't think she necessarily chose her role. It's quite possible that our vampire crossed her path casually, saw something that he liked and arranged the rest. Probably with the aid of drugs. You said that there were marks indicating that she had been bound hand and foot shortly before her death."

"Yeah."

"That doesn't necessarily mean she wasn't a willing victim, but it lends credibility to the drug theory. She was slipped a mickey, wakes up on a table somewhere with her hands and feet tied. Some sort of needle apparatus was stuck into her neck and the blood drained. The only good thing is that death was probably quick and relatively painless."

It sounded all too plausible and grim. "You think the blood was drained before she died?"

"It's not that easy to get blood out of a corpse. I asked an undertaker about it once. It was for a movie I was consulting on. With animals, they hang them up to bleed out. Whoever did it to

Anna knew what they were doing and had made preparations for it."

I shuddered at the sheer dispassionate horror of it. "What kind of person does a thing like that?"

"That's not my field. You'd need to talk to a specialist in abnormal psychology to get the answer to that question, I'm afraid. But I think the answer would be that he's nuts."

The professor was right about that.

"So does any of this ring a bell? Did something similar occur in one of your movies?"

"The problem is that vampire movies all tend to work off the same playbook. Part of the appeal is that the audience knows the rules. The aversion to garlic or holy water, the deadly affects of sunlight, no reflections in mirrors, the super human strength, the ability to turn into a bat. You keep seeing these things in movie after movie. Yet most of it bears no resemblance to the actual vampire legends. Half of it was made up by Bram Stoker, the rest was added by the writers on the Bela Lugosi movies. That's what people know, so that's what they've come to expect. Our killer probably got most of what he thinks from those same movies. With a few embellishments, Anna could be a stand in for Mina Harker."

"So that's no help?"

"Not necessarily. In Dracula, both the play and the movies based on it, the vampire bites his victim while they sleep in their own bed. That's not happened in Anna's case. It's actually more like a scene from The Blood of the Vamypre's Daughter."

"I'm afraid I missed that one," I commented.

"Too many people did, unfortunately. I consulted on the screenplay. Anyway, the intended victim is kidnapped, taken to a dungeon, laid out on an altar in a ritual meant to echo marriage, and then bitten while laying there, turning her into a vampire."

"Sounds closer to the mark."

"Maybe," Hazeltine said skeptically. "But the device has been used in other movies as well. It's sort of standard operating procedure for mad scientists. And if you're wondering, I wasn't responsible for it being used in the movie. That was one of the writer's ideas."

"So where does that leave us?"

"You tell me. You're the detective."

"From what you've told me it sounds like we've got a nut case on our hands who watched too many vampire movies as a kid and is now trying to act them out to create his very own vampire bride. Is that about the size of it?"

"Pretty much."

"Great."

"Ready for another drink?   A Bloody Mary?" Hazeltine suggested with a nervous laugh.

"Not tonight, Professor.   I'm probably going to have nightmares as it is."

On that note, I got up and left. The professor stayed an ordered another drink. I'd been right, though. I did have nightmares that night. One of them involved Anna Smerchek biting my leg where the bullet had hit it. I didn't sleep after that.

15.

When I got back to my apartment, I called Murphy. He'd made the mistake of giving me his home number. It wasn't quite ten, so I figured he'd still be up.

He answered in a voice that was both cranky and tired like he wanted to go to bed but couldn't. He might have been drinking, but if he had, it wasn't having the desired effect. Right out of the box I asked him, "Did you put a tail on Hazeltine?"

"No I didn't. Not that it's any of your business. What makes you think I did?"

"Because the professor thinks he's being followed, that's why."

"He's probably just imagining it. When did he tell you he was being followed, anyway?"

"Tonight. I ran into him in a bar."

"Look, I wouldn't get too close to the professor. You might regret it."

"What do you mean? You don't still think he had something to do with the death of the Smerchek girl, do you?"

"I can't really talk about it," Murphy answered. "The investigation is ongoing." The way he said it led me to believe that Hazeltine was his prime suspect. His only suspect.

"If you're still investigating Hazeltine, you're wasting your time. He didn't do it."

"How do you know? For that matter, how well do you know Hazeltine? You'd never met him until a month ago."

"I know him well enough to know he's not a murderer," I answered argumentatively. The fact was that Murphy had a point. I'd only spent a few hours with the professor. He had seemed straight enough to me, but there have been plenty of psychopaths that have been real good at concealing their true natures.

"Look. Certain facts have come to light about the professor," Murphy said before I had had a chance to decide how to respond.

"What kind of facts?"

"I can't tell you. It's an ongoing investigation. You were a cop long enough to know how things work."

"Don't give me that line of bull, Murphy."

"OK. Don't say I didn't warn you. But not over the phone. Come down to the department tomorrow and I'll show you what we've got. Maybe then you'll change your mind. Right now I'm going to bed." The line went dead.

Murphy seemed pretty sure of himself which had me worried. He could be bull headed at times, but he wasn't stupid. If he thought he had something on Hazeltine it was probably real.

I showed up at the police detective bureau the next morning around ten. I'd brought a couple of coffees as a peace offering. I knew what police station coffee was like.

Murphy was waiting like he had expected me. There was a thick file sitting on his desk. I set one of the coffees in front of him.

"Thanks. Have a seat." Murphy wasn't as cranky as he had been over the phone but he still sounded tired.

"So what are these facts about Hazeltine you were talking about?"

"Did he ever mention the name Marjorie Price to you?"

"No. Not that I remember."

"That's not surprising." Murphy said it with prudish disapproval.

"OK. Who is she?" I was starting to wonder if another victim had been unearthed.

"She was a graduate student in the Literature department. She and Hazeltine had an affair. She got pregnant and wanted the professor to pay for an abortion. When he didn't she filed a complaint with the university."

"What happened with the complaint?"

"No action was taken. It seems Miss Price wasn't actually a student of the professor's at the time so that in the eyes of the university there wasn't any ethical lapse."

"And how old was she?"

"Twenty-five," Murphy answered reluctantly.

"Old enough to have known better. OK. She might have been a dozen years younger than Hazeltine, but she was still of age. Hazeltine isn't married, so it wasn't even adultery on his part. As far as I'm concerned, all he's guilty of is bad judgement. Maybe not even that depending on how Miss Price looks. Maybe she came on to him? Maybe he was serious about her? It doesn't matter. If that's all you've got on Hazeltine you'll be laughed out of court."

"It's not," Murphy said. He opened the file and pulled out a couple of photos. They looked like they had been taken of pages from a book. One showed a woman in a long white dress who had been laid out on the top of an altar, her hands crossed over her breasts. The second showed a close up of what looked like a woman's neck. There were two round puncture wounds where the jugular vein is.

"Look familiar?" Murphy asked. I knew what he meant. It was a different woman, a few years older and with different colored hair, but the pose was virtually identical to that in the cellar where we'd found Anna Smerchek.

"Where'd you get these?" I asked.

"They came out of a book. *Vampyres – Fact and Fiction*. By Professor George Hazeltine. I tried to get it from the public library, but it was checked out. I ended up having to get it from another town. Remarkable how the details match those of the Smerchek case, isn't it?"

"We both know that Hazeltine has an interest in vampires and things like that. That's not a secret. He's even an authority on the subject, at least about how vampires are portrayed in books and movies. The fact that he wrote a book on the subject shows that. And it's only natural that some pictures of vampires and their victims might show up in a book like that. They don't prove anything."

"Do you know where those pictures came from?" Murphy asked. He said it like he knew the answer and I wasn't going to like it.

"No. Some movie I expect. There are hundreds of vampire movies."

"You're right. Both pictures are stills taken from the same movie. "The Blood of the Vamypre's Daughter" to be exact. Do you know who was a consultant on that movie?"

"Sure. Hazeltine. He told me himself. It's only natural that he'd use stills from that movie seeing as he was involved in it. It was probably easier to get the rights to include them in the book. But he told me that the scene wasn't his idea. It was one of the writers that thought up the idea. Those pictures don't prove anything."

"The D.A. thinks differently."

"What! All you've shown me is a bunch of circumstantial evidence, and not even good evidence at that. You can't expect to convict Hazeltine with that. Particularly as he didn't do it!"

"You still believe that?" Murphy asked. He was serious.

"Yes, I do."

"Look at it from my point of view. Or better yet, from a jury's. You've got this professor who we can demonstrate has a thing for younger women. Anna Smerchek was one of his students. She also attended his afterhours sessions. The man also seems to be obsessed with vampires and werewolves and all that creepy stuff. In fact he seems to have made a career out of that obsession. What am I supposed to think?"

I knew what was going through Murphy's mind. The D.A.'s, too. They had a high profile case and the public was clamoring for a solution. In Hazeltine they had someone they could pin it on. That would take the heat off them. It didn't matter if he was guilty or not. That was up to a jury to decide. They could go into court with a clear conscience no matter how it ended up. The responsibility rested on the judge and the jury, not them. I wasn't even sure that in their place I wouldn't have done the same thing.

"If you lock up all the men who like old movies or young women of legal age, you're going to have mighty full jails, Murphy."

"It's the D.A.'s call to make, not mine. I just thought you ought to know what was happening so you don't get caught up in it. You were a good cop until you took that bullet in the leg. That still counts for something."

From Murphy's perspective he was playing straight with me. Hell I thought, he might even be right.

"Yeah, thanks. Do you have anything else to show me?"

"No."

"Then I'll get out of your hair."

"OK. I'm counting on you not to let Hazeltine get any word of this."

"Sure," I said as I got up and left.

Two days later Professor George Hazeltine was arrested for the murder of Anna Smerchek.

16.

The press treated the story about Hazeltine's arrest about the way you'd expect. Lurid stories sell papers and get people to watch the evening news, and as the gruesome details of Anna Smerchek's death came out the newspapers played it up to the hilt. One of the first headlines I saw was "College Prof Slays Co-ed in Satanic Ritual." They didn't get any better after that. After the first flurry of articles on the crime, the reporters scrambled for details with which to fill column inches. Hazeltine's "obsession" with vampires was just the kind of fodder they were looking for. The editorial section wasn't treating him any better and there were the usual calls for heads to roll at the university. In that atmosphere it wasn't too surprising that the university essentially disowned the professor after the first press release from the D. A.'s office.

It didn't really matter that from all I could tell the case against Hazeltine was still purely circumstantial. The public's mind was made up. Even I began to question whether I had been wrong about the professor. I still didn't think that he'd done it, but I was becoming less certain of that as the days passed. After all, Hazeltine's interest in vampires and werewolves and the whole business wasn't the workings of a healthy mind, was it?

It was three days after the arrest that I got the call from Waldorf, Williams and Wohlberg. Actually it was a secretary of that firm asking if it would be convenient for me to meet with Mr. Williams at his office at two-thirty that afternoon. It didn't really matter if it was convenient or not, not for a struggling P.I. like myself. Waldorf, Williams and Wohlberg or "WWW," as they were often referred to, was one of the most important law firms in the state. They certainly weren't the biggest by any means, and they specialized almost exclusively on criminal defense, eschewing the more lucrative areas of commercial law, but if you were going to trial, and you had the money, you got one of the three partners to represent you. They didn't lose many cases, which was why their client list included many of the state's most high-profile citizens that had ever been accused of a crime. They didn't need to chase ambulances, ambulances chased them.

The secretary had declined to reveal what Williams wanted to discuss, but I had a pretty good idea that it was the Hazeltine case. In a way, I took that as a good sign. If Williams was defending the professor, he probably thought that he could get an acquittal.

For my part, it didn't matter. A private investigator needs clients, and getting on the good side of a firm like WWW was something I couldn't pass up. If Mr. Williams wanted to see me at two-thirty, that was fine with me. Even if the professor's ship was sunk, my visit might put me in the way of some good future business.

The offices of Waldorf, Williams and Wohlberg occupied the entire fourth floor of the Commercial and Business Bank building. For a defense attorney it was a great location, within easy walking distance of both the Circuit Court and Municipal buildings.

There was a parking attendant on duty who inquired if I had "business" with the bank. The way he looked at my car, he probably thought I needed a car loan. When I said that I had a meeting with Waldorf, Williams and Wohlberg he became more deferential, and directed me to a spot reserved for visitors to the firm. It was also convenient to the elevators.

I took the elevator up to the fourth floor and stepped out into the reception area. It was about what you'd expect, lots of walnut paneling and plush carpet with just enough polished brass hardware to lend a sparkle. Oil paintings of the three partners were hung on the walls looking both welcoming and wise. Just the sort of person that you'd want defending you.

The receptionist checked my name against her calendar, and when she saw I was on the list smiled and motioned me to a very comfortable chair saying someone would be with me in a moment. I'd barely gotten seated when a woman in her early thirties came for me. She was dressed in a severe gray suit, wore black rimmed glasses and had her blond hair caught up in a tight chignon, the very model of legal efficiency.

"Mr. Williams will see you now," she said in a voice not nearly as severe as her appearance.

I was ushered into Williams' office. The attorney was sitting behind a desk that was large without being overpowering. He was, in a word, distinguished looking, dark haired with just a touch of silver at the temples, silver that was so perfect I had to wonder if it was completely natural.

"Have a seat, please," Williams said. He said it with a voice that was trained to sway juries, a voice that exuded confidence and reliability. The voice alone had gotten clients off.

I took a seat in one of the leather chairs facing him. It was firm, yet comfortable. I imagined that it had been chosen to make clients feel secure yet inferior to the man behind the desk.

"I understand that you were employed as an investigator by the parents of Anna Smerchek. Is that correct?" His question wasn't hostile, but I did feel like I was being cross-examined.

"Yes."

"Are you still in their employ?"

"No. Once Anna's body was found, there didn't seem to be any point. I didn't want to take any more of their money. They'd had enough grief as it is."

"You are also acquainted with Professor Hazeltine, are you not?"

"Not really acquainted with him, Mr. Williams. I contacted him in the course of my investigation of the Smerchek case. I've talked to him several times since."

"Let me ask you a question. And I want an honest answer."

"Of course."

"Do you think that Professor Hazeltine is responsible for Anna Smerchek's death?"

I hesitated with my response. I wasn't quite sure where Williams was going with his questioning. Finally I replied.

"No. I don't think he did it."

"Despite what the police and the newspapers are saying?"

"Despite that."

"Excellent," Williams said with a smile. If I'd been a dog I would have rolled over and begged.

"You understand, Mr. Williams, that's just my personal opinion."

"But one that I value, I assure you."

"I take it you're defending the professor?"

"That is correct."

"If you don't mind my asking, sir, aren't your rates a little steep for a college professor?"

Williams gave a little laugh. "I see I haven't misjudged you. You are correct, the fees of Waldorf, Williams and Wohlberg are steep, though an excellent value, I might add. However, it turns out that Professor Hazeltine has some friends in the movie and publishing industry with deep pockets."

"That's good to hear."

"You like the professor, don't you?" It was a question this time, not an interrogation.

"Yeah. He's a bit odd for my tastes, but he's just an ordinary guy when you come right down to it. I think he played straight with me and I'd hate to see him get a raw deal."

"So would I. So would I. Tell me, what do you think of the case against him? I understand you know the detective on the case?"

"Yeah. Murphy. He's a good cop, but I think he's wrong on this one. All the evidence against Hazeltine is circumstantial at best. Anna Smerchek was one of his students the semester before her disappearance. It was a big class, over two hundred students I believe. She attended some of his afterhours sessions, but so did a lot of other students. Other than that there's no evidence of any contact between them that I'm aware of."

"The police are making much of similarities between the scene where Anna's body was found and scenes in a movie that the professor was involved with. What do you think of that? You were present when the body was discovered I believe?"

"Not when it was discovered, but I was there before the body had been moved. I've seen the stills that the D.A. is using, too. Yeah, there are similarities between the two. I'll grant you that, but that doesn't mean Hazeltine killed her. He told me he hadn't had anything to do with that scene in the movie, anyhow."

"You've talked with Professor Hazeltine?"

"Yeah, we met for a drink a couple days before he was arrested. He knew that Murphy was investigating him. He was pretty shook up about that."

"As well he should have been. Tell me, what do you think explains the similarities between the crime scene and the movie?"

"When it comes down to it there are only so many ways to lay a body out on a table. The way it was done is kind of the natural way, almost like it would be done in a funeral parlor. Body straight, hands crossed over the breast. Maybe it can be done other ways, like laying on the side, curled up, I'm no expert on that kind of thing, but the way she was found is the simplest way."

"The police are saying there is more to the similarities than that. It was almost as if whoever was responsible was trying to recreate the scene. Hence their interest in Professor Hazeltine."

"I don't know. Maybe the killer saw the movie. Maybe he read the book. Somebody must have. It was checked out of the library when I tried to look at it."

"You tried to check out the book?" Williams asked with some surprise.

"Yeah, when I was first checking out Hazeltine. I wanted to get some background on him before I interviewed him."

"That is interesting. Why did you interview the professor in the first place?"

"Because of something Anna's sister told me. She mentioned that Anna had talked to her about a professor that she had really liked, Hazeltine. So I wanted to check him out. Not that her sister implied anything sexual. Just that Anna found what he was teaching interesting."

"And this was about vampires?"

"No. Just world literature. It was all new to Anna. You have to understand that she came from a small town up north. You know the kind of place, all Germans and Norwegians with maybe a few Polacks and Bohunks thrown in for seasoning. Anything else would have seemed exotic."

"And you interviewed Hazeltine?"

"Yeah. And I pretty much ruled him out afterwards. He just didn't seem the type."

"And just what do you think the type would be?"

"Me. I think the guy that killed Anna Smerchek is nuts. I think he really believes he is a vampire."

"And do you have any suspects in mind?"

"There's one guy I ran across in the investigation. He goes by the name Vladimir Romanesu. He runs an occult book store, dresses in black and talks in a Bela Lugosi accent. Anna went to a lecture at his store at least once not too long before she disappeared."

"And what do the police think about this Romanescu? I assume you told them about him?"

"Yeah. I told Murphy. He said he checked the place out, but didn't find anything suspicious. Maybe he didn't have anything to do with Anna, but he was still kind of creepy."

"I see. Hardly evidence, but perhaps this Romanescu bears looking into. Which brings me to the second reason I wanted to see you. Would you have any objections to acting as an investigator on Professor Hazeltine's behalf?"

"Why would I?"

"You were employed by Anna Smerchek's parents. You might feel there was an ethical conflict."

"No. Not if Hazeltine didn't do it. Vern Smerchek asked me to find who killed his daughter after I told him she was dead. If Hazeltine didn't kill her, someone else did. I'd like to find out who."

"Good. Consider yourself hired then. My secretary Miss Philips will arrange the details and see that you get an advance to cover expenses. I'd like to find out some more about this Vladimir Romanescu. What his background is, that sort of thing. Of course, we have staff to handle the routine inquiries, but I think you might have other avenues available to you."

"That makes sense."

"There is one other thing. You said Hazeltine's book was checked out of the library."

"Yeah. The funny thing is that it was checked out when Murphy tried to get it, too. He had to get a copy from another city."

"It might be interesting to find out who else has checked out the book. Do you think you can manage that?"

"Sure."

"Then I think it's time for you to get to work. I look forward to hearing from you."

He pressed a button on his desk and Miss Philips came to escort me out.

17.

I left the offices of Waldorf, Williams and Wohlberg with a thousand dollar check in my pocket. More importantly, Miss Philips had kindly typed out a letter on the firm's stationary proclaiming that I was investigating at the behest of the firm and requesting that anyone who read the letter should offer me any assistance possible. I was starting to feel a lot more positive about Hazeltine's chances of avoiding a conviction.

My conversation with Williams had taken less than an hour which still left me some time in the day. The question was how best to spend it. Williams had been interested in who had checked out the library's copy of Hazeltine's book, *Vampyres – Fact and Fiction*. I wasn't quite sure why, but then I'm not a lawyer. Maybe he thought it was a way to divert suspicion from the professor. What I did know was that if Williams was interested, it would pay me to be interested, too. A visit to the public library seemed as good a use of what remained of the afternoon as anything else.

As I walked past the front desk I noted that the librarian on duty was the same one that had helped me on my previous visit. I gave her a nod and a smile which she returned with some amusement.

A quick check of the shelves showed me that the book was still checked out. I returned to the front desk.

"I was wondering if you could help me. I'm looking for a book, *Vampyres – Fact and Fiction*, by George Hazeltine. I've checked the shelves, but it seems to be checked out."

The librarian looked a little surprised when I mentioned the title. She must have been hoping that I read more serious works.

"I could place a hold on it and notify you when it's returned," she said professionally.

"The thing is, the last time I was in here to look for it, the book was also not on the shelf. Is there any way you could check on its status? It's rather important."

I could sense that she was starting to wonder if I was some kind of crank who was going to cause trouble.

"Perhaps I should explain myself. I'm a private investigator and I'm a interested in the book for a case."

"Oh," she responded a little disconcerted.

"Here is my state license. I also have a letter from the attorney that I'm working for." Miss Philips had informed me that Wohlberg's wife was on the library's board of trustees. Glancing at the letterhead, it was apparent that the librarian was also aware of the fact.

"I see. Just exactly is it that you want me to do?"

"First, if possible, I'd like to discover the status of the book. Whether it really is checked out or not. I hate to impose, but it is of some importance."

"I can check our records. It may take a few minutes."

"I'd appreciate that. I've got plenty of time."

She disappeared into a back room leaving me leaning on the desk. I was getting curious looks from some of the patrons at the tables, but that didn't bother me. I'm used to getting curious looks.

The librarian returned after five minutes or so. She seemed unhappy.

"It's very odd, but it seems that the book has been out quite some time."

"Oh? How long?"

"Well, I hate to admit it, but it was checked out over a year ago and never returned." She seemed upset at the fact that her ordered world had been upset.

"Does that kind of thing happen often?" I asked sympathetically.

"No, not often, but it does happen. Usually people just forget they have a book. Once a book is more than two weeks past due we send out a notice. Most people will return the item when they receive a notice. If not, we send another notice after another month."

"And if that doesn't work?"

"We suspend the library card of the individual."

"And quite properly, too. I suppose that procedure was followed in the case of this book?"

"Yes. The problem is that the first notice was returned as undeliverable. Of course, we still sent the second notice, but that was returned by the post office as well."

"That's unfortunate."

"Yes. Some people just have no sense of responsibility."

"I quite agree. When exactly was the book checked out that last time?"

"Let see," she said referring to the card she held in her hand. "It was August 18th of last year."

That was a good three months before Anna Smerchek had been killed. I was beginning to see why Williams had been interested. If it could be shown that someone was interested enough in the book to steal it from the library, that fact could be used to sway a jury into thinking that Hazeltine wasn't the only person with a vampire obsession.

"Just out of curiosity, what happens when a book goes missing? Does the library replace it?" I wasn't really interested in the answer, but I was trying to distract the librarian from the question that I was really interested in.

"It depends," the librarian answered thoughtfully. "If the book is an important one or popular, then a replacement will be purchased. However, if the book is an older one or of more specialized interest, then we may choose not to replace it. Unfortunately, we only have a limited budget for acquisitions."

"Quite understandable. I take it that in this case a replacement has not been purchased?"

"That would be correct. We might have to rethink that, though. Yours is not the first request for the book recently."

I knew that Murphy had tried to get the book, but with the notoriety the case had been getting, I wasn't surprised that others had sought it out. The title had gotten extensive coverage in the press. Of course, that kind of interest tends to have a fairly short lifespan.

"I'd hold off, if I were you."

The librarian looked at me quizzically.

"Is there any chance that I could get the name and address of the last person to check the book out?"

"I really shouldn't. The privacy of our patrons is important."

"Of course. Though the circumstances in this instance are a little different. I don't want to cause you any trouble, and I can, of course, get a court order, if that is necessary. I'd like to safe us both some trouble, though, if at all possible."

"Since you put it that way, I suppose I could make an exception. It's not as though the person still lives at the address. Who knows, the name on the card might not even be a real one."

"You don't require proof of identity before giving out a library card?" I hadn't really thought about it, before. My own card I'd had since I was a kid.

"This isn't a bank," she said, with a note of regret. "We largely operate on the honor system."

"Of course. You were going to give me the name and address?"

She turned the card around so that I could read it. "Coleen Smith, 449 E. Walden St." I wrote down the information in my notebook.

"I'd like to thank you for your cooperation, Miss—"

"Weston, Ellen Weston."

"Miss Weston. I want to assure you that unless the information is required for trial I won't mention the source. And thanks again."

"Good-bye."

It was curious. She seemed relieved to get rid of me, but a bit disappointed that the excitement was over. I suppose librarians don't get that many opportunities to break out of the routine.

On my way home, I checked out the address Coleen Smith had used on her library card. It turned out to be a vacant lot.

18.

I spent the next couple of days getting frustrated trying to get a handle on Romanescu. A search of the publicly accessible records turned up absolutely nothing. As far as they told me he hadn't been born, hadn't married, and he hadn't died, at least not in this state. He was listed as the owner of record for the building where the House of Esoteric Wisdom was located, and he had taken out the necessary business license for the book store. The property taxes on the building had been paid promptly in each of the last three years. Other than that, Romanescu might as well not have existed.

I did manage to track down the realtor that had handled the sale of the building to Romanescu. Not that that did me much good. It was, as the realtor explained, "a few years back," and he couldn't really remember any of the details other than the fact that the buyer had been "kind of foreign" sounding. When I consulted his records, all they revealed was the fact that the transaction had been closed with a check drawn on an out-of-state bank. The check had cleared with no problems. The paperwork listed no previous permanent address for Romanescu. The contact information was for a room at a motel on the edge of town that offered reduced rates for rooms taken by the week. When I asked the realtor if that was unusual he had shrugged. He dealt with a lot of rental properties near the campus and was used to deals where the prospective buyer provided few details about themselves. As long as the money was good he didn't care.

The bank Romanescu had written the check on was located in Columbus, Ohio. The only information they would divulge was the fact that Romanescu no longer maintained an account with them. I passed the information along to Waldorf, Williams, and Wohlberg through Miss Philips on the theory that they had better resources to follow up the lead than I did. That might have been true, but they weren't having much better luck uncovering the details of Romanescu's life than I was, at least according to Miss Philips.

I spent some time looking through newspaper archives, as well, but Romanescu and the House of Esoteric Wisdom never made an appearance in print, at least in the last three years. The man dressed in black was proving to be very good at keeping a low profile.

It was along about this time that I got a call from Murphy saying he wanted to meet. He didn't say what he wanted, but I agreed to see him for a beer at The Dead End after the end of his shift.

I was a little late, and Murphy was at the bar sipping on a beer. I grabbed the stool next to him and told the bartender to pour me the same. After it came I asked, "So what's up?"

"I hear that you're working for Hazeltine's lawyer."

"Oh. Where'd you hear that?"

I was surprised. I certainly hadn't been spreading the word around. I couldn't necessarily see Williams giving out the information either, let alone Miss Philips.

"From the D. A.'s office."

"It must be true then," I said sarcastically.

"Are you?"

"Yeah." I didn't see any point in denying the fact. It was clear that Murphy believed it. Besides, it was true.

"Do you really think that your professor is innocent?" There was an edge of betrayal in the policeman's voice.

"Of killing Anna Smerchek? Yeah, I do."

"In spite of the evidence?"

"What evidence? Hazeltine teaches a popular course. He worked on a vampire film. Okay, he's a little nuts on the subject, maybe. Werewolves, too, but he doesn't go around howling at the full moon. But real hard physical evidence? There's nothing tying him to Anna Smerchek or the crime scene. The D. A. is going to have a real hard time selling his case to a jury. Especially once a lawyer like Williams starts working on him."

Murphy was silent, then. He knew that what I had said was true even if he didn't like it. He just stared into his beer for awhile. Me, I drank mine and ordered another.

"Okay. So if the professor didn't do it who do you think killed her?"

"I don't know, but I'd put my money on Romanescu before Hazeltine any day. Why haven't you guys checked him out?"

"We have. We didn't find anything."

"How hard did you look? Did you get a search warrant to check out the basement of that Esoteric Wisdom place?"

"I didn't have to. After you brought up the fact that Anna had been there I went and checked it out. Romanescu was very cooperative. He let me check out the place from top to bottom. There was nothing. No altar in the cellar, no dungeon, just a lot of weird books and cheap furniture."

"So Anna was killed someplace else. Romanescu is a smooth operator, too smooth to do something like that where it could be traced back to him. What did he say about Anna having been there?"

"He said he didn't remember her, but that a lot of college kids drop in once or twice. When I showed him her picture he said she looked vaguely familiar but that was all. The same with Coleen."

"Coleen?" I asked. The name was familiar, but I couldn't make the connection.

"Yeah. Coleen. The girl that works the book store. I showed her a picture of Anna. She said that she thought that she'd been at one of the lectures, but she couldn't say when. She might have come back a day or two later to browse the book store, but as far as she could remember, she hadn't bought anything."

"And you believed them?"

"Admit it, you just don't like Romanescu because he's creepy and it would be a lot easier for you to believe that he did it than your professor."

"He's not my professor. And I could say the same thing about you and Hazeltine."

"Look, let's not argue about this."

"Fine by me. Why did you want to see me, anyhow?"

"When the D. A. told me you were working for the defense I was surprised. I really thought that you wanted to get whoever killed the Smerchek girl."

"I do. Believe me, I do."

"I knew that you thought that Hazeltine was innocent and this Romanescu was a prime suspect. I just wanted to tell you that we'd checked him out and didn't find anything. If Romanescu didn't do it, maybe you'll rethink Hazeltine."

"So what did you find out about Romanescu's background?"

"Not much. He doesn't have a criminal record. He said he was born in Hungary, but because of the communist government there was no way to confirm that. He'd been involved in anti-government activity and just managed to escape. That's why he keeps a low profile in case Hungarian agents try to kill him or take him back."

"And you believed that story? Did you check with the State Department?"

"I checked. They didn't admit to anything other than that Romanescu is in the country legally."

"That's reassuring. For all you know he could be a spy or a double agent or something. And it wouldn't be the first time our government covered up the dirty past of someone because they wanted to use them."

"Look, I'm just trying to tell you what I know, and none of it points to Romanescu as the killer."

"Fine. But that still doesn't mean that Hazeltine is."

"Maybe not, but no other suspects have surfaced."

I took a long pull of my beer. I didn't really want to argue with Murphy. At heart he was a good cop even if a little pigheaded at times. I changed the subject.

"Have you had any luck on finding out where Anna actually was killed? You're sure it wasn't the cellar where she was found?"

"No, she was killed someplace else. Forensics is sure about that. But we haven't found it yet."

"My guess is it would have to be close. You wouldn't want to have to carry a body too far."

"You're probably right, but there are all sorts of old buildings in that neighborhood, and half of them are empty. It's not the best part of town. And whoever killed her has had plenty of time to clean up."

"And leave town."

"Yeah. That would have been the smart thing to do."

My beer was empty, and I didn't feel like sitting there drinking and arguing with Murphy. It was pretty clear that we were both frustrated by the case, and without new evidence neither one of us was going to change our minds.

"Thanks for the information, Murphy. It's getting late, so I should get going. Let's just agree to disagree and leave it at that. At least until something more definitive turns up."

"Yeah. See you around," Murphy said turning back to the bar. My leg was aching so I was slow in leaving. At the door I looked back and saw Murphy ordering another beer.

Out of habit when I got home I checked in with my answering service. Miss Philips had left a message for me. I was to catch a plane the next morning for Columbus and follow up on Romanescu. Tickets and information would be waiting for me at the airport.

19.

Along with the airline tickets Miss Philips had arranged, there was also an envelope waiting for me at the ticket counter the next morning. The fact that the ticket clerk was willing to deal with anything other than airline business was evidence of the pull that Waldorf, Williams and Wohlberg had.

I boarded the plane, stowed my overnight bag and buckled myself into my seat. I'm not a big fan of flying. It's not that I'm afraid, it's just that I find it noisy and uncomfortable.

The flight to Columbus is a little over two hours. After the takeoff I split the seal on the envelope and took out the contents. It was a report from a local P.I. agency in Columbus that Williams had hired to check out Romanescu. It ran to about a dozen pages, but could have been condensed into one. It appeared that wherever Romanescu had traveled he had made a habit of maintaining a low profile. The gist of the report was that he had maintained an account at the bank that we had already known about. He had opened the account with a large deposit in the form of a check drawn on a New York state bank ten years back. Within a few months of opening the account he had withdrawn most of the money to purchase an older house near the Ohio State campus. He had sold that property and deposited the proceeds into the account several months before he had moved on. It was that money that he had used to purchase the building for the House of Esoteric Wisdom. Other than that, the local detective hadn't been able to unearth much about Romanescu's stay in Columbus.

The Columbus airport could have been the airport for any medium size Midwestern city. At mid day it was nearly empty except for those passengers arriving on the same flight that I had and a few bored counter clerks in the check in area. It was a little warmer than when I'd taken off, but not much. Just a normal late spring day.

The detective from the local agency was waiting for me. There'd been a note to that effect in the envelope. I didn't have any trouble spotting him, he looked like a private dick. We could have been twins.

He had a car waiting in the airport parking lot, a Ford sedan that looked like it might have been an ex police cruiser. Old habits die hard I guess.

"So what's with this Romanescu guy, anyway?" he asked after we'd driven out of the airport. "Your boss didn't give me much in the way of background, just that he wanted any information I could dig up. Which wasn't much."

"You're right. I read your report. Don't feel bad. I didn't come up with any more when I looked into his more recent past."

"So what gives? Who is he?" the local guy persisted.

"Williams is defending a college professor on a charge of homicide. Romanescu is another possible suspect. At least it's my guess that that's the way he's going to present it to the jury."

"Do you think he did it? Romanescu I mean, not the professor."

"I don't know. Maybe. I know the professor, and I don't think he's guilty. Problem is there isn't any physical evidence pointing to either one of them."

"Tough."

"Yeah. Did you find out anything else about Romanescu that wasn't in the report? Like what he did for a living?"

"Not really. He took out a business license for a book store. I gathered that he ran it out of the property he bought. It didn't seem to make much money, though. Not enough to live on."

"What kind of book store? Do you know?"

"The license didn't specify. I asked around some of the neighbors, but you know that kind of neighborhood. Mostly rentals, college kids. The population turns over every year. I did talk to one old lady, though, that remembered the place. She didn't care for it. Claimed the books were all about black magic and witchcraft. Of course I think she was a little crazy. Probably would have said that about anything that wasn't Presbyterian. I checked with some buddies on the force. None of them could remember any complaints."

"Sounds a lot like what he's doing now," I commented.

"So why do you think this guy might be a murder suspect?"

"No real reason except that Romanescu gives me the creeps. He dresses in black and talks like Bela Lugosi."

"That sounds like the basis for a case," the local P.I. said sarcastically.

"The murdered girl had visited the book store at least once, maybe more right before she disappeared, but other than that, there's no evidence to tie the two together. The police searched the book store and didn't find anything."

"Look, I'm not complaining," the local guy said. "I don't mind chauffeuring you around as long as Williams is paying my hourly rate. It's better than most of what I do. It just seems a waste of time and money."

"It probably is," I agreed. "The case against the professor is pretty weak, all circumstantial with no real evidence other than the fact that the girl was one of his students. The D.A. brought the indictment mostly because of public pressure. The victim was a college girl from a small town up north and the details of the crime were pretty lurid. The D.A. had to do something. I think Williams' strategy is to convince the D.A. that he'll look like an idiot if he takes it to trial and hope that the charges will be dropped. Presenting a plausible alternate killer might be enough."

"Lawyers," the local man said derisively. "But as long as they're paying the bills what do I care. So, what do you want to do first?"

"Do you have the address of the place Romanesu owned? We could drive past there first."

"Sure thing."

We drove in silence for awhile, which suited me just fine. I tended to agree with my driver's opinion that the trip was a waste of time, but then that came with being a P.I.

To make conversation my driver said "You mentioned that this murder case was kind of lurid. What did you mean?"

I explained about how Anna Smerchek's body had been found.

"I can see why the pressure is on the D.A.," the local man responded. "That's just the kind of thing that gets the populace wound up. Funny thing, though, It kind of sounds like a case we had here a while back. Must have been four or five years ago. A young girl, about eighteen or so disappeared. They found her body in an abandoned meat packing plant hanging upside down. Her neck vein had been slit and the blood drained out. Pretty gruesome stuff."

"Did they ever catch whoever was responsible?"

"Nah. They tried to pin it on some drifter they caught near the packing plant, but he hung himself in his jail cell before it went to trial. The prosecutor called the case closed, but most people didn't buy into it. He lost the next election, but the new guy doesn't want to reopen the case without new evidence. Can't say I blame him."

I was about to ask for more details, but we had pulled up to the curb in front of an old Victorian house.

"This is the place," my driver said, "the one that Romanescu owned."

It had been built maybe twenty years earlier than the one that housed The House of Esoteric Wisdom, but other than that it was about the same size, two and a half stories with a broad porch across the front. This one seemed in better shape, though. It looked like it had recently been painted and the windows had fresh putty and glazing.

"Know who owns it now?"

"Some young couple, I think. He works at the university. No connection to Romanescu."

I didn't see much point in bothering the current owners.

"Where to next?"

I hadn't a clue. On a whim I said, "the public library."

I spent the first half-hour checking through directories looking for Romanescus. Other than the six years Vladimir had been in town there weren't any. I figured the local investigator had searched all the public records already so I didn't bother. That left the local newspapers.

I paged through the headlines until I found the case the local man had mentioned. The details were different, mostly. The girl had been found in a white dress but the other ceremonial aspects were missing. The blood had been drained through a cut made by a sharp knife or a scalpel, apparently at the scene where the body had been found, because there were blood spatters on the concrete floor underneath where she had been hung. It didn't appear to be the work of the same killer. Or was it just that he had spent the last four years refining his technique and rationale?

It had all happened a few months before Romanescu had sold his house and moved on. Was that just a coincidence?

I got the librarian to make me copies of the articles with the most details and stuffed them in the envelope with the report on Romanescu.

I'd let the local man take off after he'd dropped me at the library, so I took a taxi to the hotel where Miss Philips had made a reservation for me. After checking in I had a quick shower followed by a steak, baked potato and a beer in the hotel restaurant. That was followed by a rye on the rocks in the bar. I thought about another, but the place was empty except for me and the bartender, and depressing as only a empty hotel bar can be. After one drink I went up to my room with a cheap paperback that I had bought in the lobby gift shop. In the morning I took the hotel shuttle to the airport to take the morning flight back.

20.

My flight out of Columbus was delayed three hours due to a line of thunderstorms stretching south from Lake Michigan. That gave me three hours sitting in the non-descript terminal to think about Romanescu. Not that there was much to think about. The one thing that struck me was that when he had bought the house in Columbus he had either been very young at the time or he was a lot older than he looked.

The fact that we didn't even know his age was a sign of how elusive Romanescu's past was. None of the few official records we had unearthed gave an age or date of birth. As far as I or the local man had determined, Romanescu had never applied for a driver's license. Presumably his income tax returns would have the information, but that wasn't the kind of thing readily obtainable, not without probable cause, and suspecting a man of thinking he was a vampire was not probable cause. Romanescu's origins still remained a mystery when the boarding call was given.

It was late afternoon when the plane finally landed. It had been a rough flight because of the weather, and I think everybody on the plane was relieved when we touched down. I didn't see any point in going to the office, so I headed home. I would check in with Miss Philips in the morning.

I did call the answering service. Vern Smerchek had called several times while I was in Columbus. I really didn't want to talk to the man. I didn't have anything to say.

Pizza and a beer at the mom and pop pizzeria down the street from my apartment made me feel a little better, but not much. I went home planning to finish the cheap novel I had bought in Ohio. It was about a private detective who actually figured out who the bad guys were. And then proceeded to fill them full of lead without bothering with niceties like a judge or jury. That certainly would keep things simple.

I had just finished it when the phone rang. It was about nine thirty. I was surprised because I have an unlisted number and I don't usually give it out to clients. One of the rare exceptions had been to Vern Smerchek. I knew that I shouldn't answer it, but I did anyway.

"I thought I could trust you." I recognized Vern Smerchek's voice, though it sounded as if he had been drinking. I could almost smell the scent of cheap brandy through the phone. He hadn't struck me as a guy who drank much or very often, but he definitely had been drinking and he wasn't handling it well.

"It's late, Mr. Smerchek. What is this about?"

"Is it true?"

"Is what true?"

"That you're working for the man that killed my Anna?"

"Who told you that?" I wasn't going to deny the fact that I was working for the defense, but I wanted to find out who had told Smerchek.

"The man from the District Attorney's office. He called to tell me how the case was going and he told me that you were working for Hazeltine's lawyer."

"Mr. Smerchek, I'm a private investigator. That's what I do for a living. A lot of my clients are lawyers."

"But I hired you to find the man that killed my Anna. And now you're working for the man that killed her."

It had been a long day and I was starting to get mad. Belligerent drunks annoy me. Even if they have a reason to be drunk.

"First off, you hired me to find Anna. I did that. You never gave me money to find out who killed her, and I never asked you to. Second, I don't think Hazeltine is the man who killed your daughter, and thirdly, even if he did, he's entitled to a defense. That's what I'm doing. It's up to a jury to decide if he's guilty or not, not you or me."

"He's got some big shot lawyer who will get him off. And you're helping him," Smerchek slurred in response.

"Look Mr. Smerchek. If I wasn't doing this job, someone else would be, someone who might be more interested in a fee than justice. Think about that. And I've still got to eat. Besides, like I said, I don't think Professor Hazeltine killed your daughter, and if he didn't do it, someone else did. There isn't a shred of physical evidence tying Hazeltine to the crime, and you can get the D.A. to confirm that."

"But I trusted you." Smerchek was getting to that point where drunks get where they start repeating themselves. "You were going to find who killed my Anna."

"I'm sorry you feel that way, Mr. Smerchek. I really want to find the man responsible for Anna's death, you have to believe me, but it isn't Hazeltine. I think it would be best if you didn't call me again."

There was a sound from the phone that sounded like a sob. If I had been smart, I would have just hung up, but I did feel like I owed the man something. Besides, if anyone had a reason to drink, it was him. Finally he said, "She was all that I have."

"You still have a wife and another daughter, Mr. Smerchek. Think about them."

"Ellen hasn't been the same since—and Katie, she's just a tramp. Anna was the good thing in my life. I should never have let her go away to college."

"You can't hold on to your kids forever, Vern. It doesn't work that way. If you try, you both end up losing in the end." I felt a sham trying to give advice about something I had no experience with to a man I hardly knew, but I could tell that Smerchek was teetering on the ragged edge. I didn't want to be the one that pushed him over it. "You should be thankful for what you still have, Mr. Smerchek. I know it hurts now, but give it time."

There was more silence pouring from the phone then he said, "Promise me."

"Promise you what?"

"That you'll find whoever killed my Anna."

"I promise." Even at the time I didn't think it was a lie.

"Truly?"

"You have my word, Mr. Smerchek."

"I'm sorry for what I said earlier. I've been drinking. I don't usually do that. I'm guess I'm not used to it."

"I understand, Vern. Look, it's late. You should go to bed and try and get some sleep.   Things will look different in the morning."

"You promised, remember."

"Yes, I promised. Good night Mr. Smerchek."

I waited until he'd hung up and then put down the phone.

21.

I turned what information I had picked up in Columbus over to Miss Philips along with a report and an account of hours spent for billing purposes. I wasn't used to working so many hours at a time so I didn't even bother to pad the numbers. The report mentioned the coincidence of the girl from the meat packing plant. Miss Philips said that she found that very interesting and that she would mention it to Mr. Williams. She would also arrange for inquiries to be made as to Romanescu's life previous to his time in Columbus. She seemed pleased. I was happy with that. She also arranged for a check to be cut to cover time and expenses to date. I was even happier.

The next few days were quiet ones. There wasn't much to do on the case. Vern Smercheck didn't make any more phone calls, either. I spent some time in the library on my own dime reading back issues of east coast papers working back from the time that Romanescu moved to Ohio. I found plenty of accounts of mayhem and depravity, but nothing that seemed to relate to the case.

My inactivity ended when I got a call from Miss Philips asking me to meet Mr. Williams at the county jail. He had arranged a conference with the professor and wanted me to be present.

The county jail is a rather grim annex to the court house, a hideous example of post war modernism whose unadorned concrete contrasted starkly with the neo-classical limestone façade of the court house. The high narrow windows set in the blank grey walls made the place look like a citadel designed to repel the barbarian hordes, though the real intent, of course, was to keep the hordes inside.

I arrived early, stated my purpose to the jailer manning the reception desk and was told to take a seat in the waiting area. This consisted of a room about eight by twelve feet with cheap plastic chairs set against both walls. The walls were painted that shade of bilious green that is only used by hospitals and prisons. The flooring was faded linoleum of indeterminate color. There were no magazines to distract those unfortunate enough to have to sit there and the only decoration was a large poster on one wall listing the rules for visitors to the jail and promising dire consequences for those who transgressed them.

Fortunately Williams arrived within five minutes. The jailer treated the counsel with a great deal more respect than he had me. Williams motioned me to join him, and we were buzzed through a locked door into the confines of the jail proper. I admit that the insides of jails always depresses me and I try to avoid them as much as possible. Once inside, a warder escorted us to the room set aside for interviews between inmates and their lawyers.

This room was not much bigger than the waiting area. The furnishings consisted of a heavy table bolted to the floor, a metal chair, also bolted to the floor, on one side of the table intended for the prisoner, and several plastic chairs of the same model as those in the waiting area on the other side for the counsels. There were two doors to the room, one for inmates and one for visitors from outside. A large window providing a view to a dingy corridor destroyed any illusion of privacy.

Williams took one of the plastic seats, opened up his briefcase, and began examining some papers. He hadn't said a word to me. I took the other seat and waited.

A few minutes later Hazeltine was escorted in. He was wearing handcuffs. I hadn't seen him since his arrest. He didn't look good. His cheeks had hollowed out and his skin had gone the grey that people who never see the sun get. There was a fading bruise just under his left eye.

The professor seemed surprised at my presence and strangely, pleased.

"Forgive me if I don't shake your hand," Hazeltine said by way of a greeting. "It is my understanding that it is against the rules."

"How have you been?" I asked knowing how lame it sounded.

"As well as can be expected. They've had me in solitary confinement for my own protection. It seems some of the other inmates of this asylum took exception to my alleged crimes." His hands went up to the bruise on his face. He didn't sound so much bitter as resigned.

"I'm sorry about that." In a way, I felt responsible for the professor's plight. If I hadn't gone poking around in the case, he might not have become involved.

"It's not your fault. Besides, you appear to be the only real friend I have. None of my colleagues have visited or even tried to contact me. I've become something of a pariah in university circles it appears. At least the movie people have provided some funds for Mr. Williams here."

Turning to Williams he said, "Is there any chance that you've arranged to get me out of this hell hole?"

"Unfortunately, Professor, bail is not possible for first degree homicide in this state. Given the flimsy nature of the evidence against you, I've been trying to persuade the prosecutor to drop the charges, but the D. A. has backed himself into a corner on this case by promising the public that the culprit in the Smerchek case is behind bars. To admit that he has made a mistake would seriously jeopardize his chances for reelection."

"Well you can tell him he's lost my vote," Hazeltine commented. "So where does that put me?"

"I have every confidence that if the case goes to trial we will prevail. However, the case isn't scheduled to go before a judge for three months."

"So I'm stuck here for at least that long?"

"Once a judge is assigned the case, I will, of course, make a motion for a dismissal of all charges on the grounds of lack of evidence. Depending on the judge, that might succeed."

"And if not?"

"We go to trial. Believe me, the full resources of Waldorf, Williams, and Wohlberg will be used in your defense."

"I appreciate that, Mr. Williams. I really do. But from my side of the table things are looking pretty bleak."

"Oh, I wouldn't lose heart, Professor. Your friend here has been working diligently on your behalf. He's managed to turn up some interesting information about this Vladimir Romanescu, information that may well convince a jury that someone other than yourself was responsible for the unfortunate death of Anna Smerchek. Remember, all we need introduce is a reasonable doubt."

"I'd settle for some unreasonable doubt at this point."

"We may, in fact, have some. Your friend has turned up some details on a case that bears a resemblance to the one at hand. A girl that was murdered in Columbus, Ohio around five years ago. I don't suppose you were ever in Columbus in that time frame."

"Not to my recollection."

"Could you prove that?"

"Maybe. That was the year I took a sabbatical to work on *Blood of the Vampyre's Daughter*. I also was on a publicity tour for my book. That was mostly the coasts with stops in Chicago, New Orleans and Austin, Texas. My publisher could probably provide the details. Why? Is it important?"

"Why don't you fill in the professor as to what you found?"

"There was a case in Columbus. A girl about eighteen went missing and was later found hanging upside down in an abandoned meat packing plant. She was wearing a white dress and all of her blood had been drained."

"Gruesome, but I don't see the relevance."

"Vladimir Romanescu was living in Columbus at the time. It was shortly after that that he moved here."

"So you're planning to pin the crime on this Romanescu? What if he didn't do it?   I'd hate to put someone through what I've experienced if they're innocent."

"We're not trying to prove the guilt of anyone, professor," Williams assured him. "All we're trying to do is establish a 'reasonable doubt' and show that the police did not do due diligence in investigating the crime and all possible suspects. It is my understanding that the investigation of Mr. Romanescu was rather cursory and consisted of a single interview and a rather brief search of his place of business months after the actual murder had occurred."

"I'm still not sure I'm comfortable with that," Hazeltine said.

"That's the way the game is played, Professor. Trust me. I have far greater experience in this area than you do. Believe me, if your prosecution fails, the D. A. will be reluctant to charge someone else without a water tight case. He won't want to be made to look the fool twice. This Romanescu will not be charged unless he really is the guilty party."

"I guess I've placed myself in your hands, Mr. Williams. I'll have to trust your judgement."

"Good. I'm glad that's settled. Now is there anything else I can do for you? Anything I can get you?"

"I'd appreciate some decent reading material. The jail library leaves a lot to be desired."

"If you will send Miss Philips a list, I'll see what can be done. I think that will be all for the moment. We'll be in touch with your publisher and the movie studio about your whereabouts at the time of the Columbus murder. Keep your spirits up, Professor Hazeltine. Good day."

Williams packed up his briefcase and stood. A warder must have been watching, because someone came to escort Hazeltine out. A moment later our own escort appeared.

Once outside of the jail Williams asked, "Could you walk with me to my car?"

"I'd like to thank you. That case you unearthed in Columbus was most fortuitous."

"Do you think it really has anything to do with the Smerchek murder?"

"Who knows," he said with a shrug. "What matters is what a jury will think. Please don't think me cynical. You think the professor is innocent and so do I. My job is to convince a jury of that by any means possible, even if it means getting them to believe in non-existent connections. I won't lose any sleep over the fact as long as my client is judged not guilty."

"Oh, I understand that, alright," I replied.

"Good. Let me ask you a question. Do you really think this Romanescu is the one who killed Anna Smerchek?"

"Maybe. I don't know. There's something about him. It's just a feeling. I don't have any real facts to back it up, but I've learned to trust my gut."

"Don't underestimate your intuition. On another matter, I understand that you know the investigating officer, Sergeant Murphy. Is that correct?"

"Yeah. A little bit. We're not friends but we talk."

"It just might be beneficial to instill a little doubt in his mind. You might drop a hint about the Columbus case in his ear."

We'd reached his car, a new Cadillac. "I'll be in touch," Williams said as he slid behind the wheel.

22.

The people Williams had hired to find Romanescu's antecedents had drawn a blank. I wasn't familiar with the investigators that he'd hired, but he wouldn't have hired them if they didn't know their business. If Romanescu had lived on the east coast ten to fifteen years earlier, he hadn't been using the name Romanescu. This didn't really help the cause much, it just deepened the mystery surrounding the man in black.

Hazeltine's case was assigned a judge and given a tentative date for trial. In due course Williams made his motion for dismissal on the grounds of lack of evidence. It was promptly turned down as was a motion for bail.

On the day that the professor spent his sixtieth day in jail I decided to take Williams advice and called up Murphy. He seemed surprised, but agreed to meet me at The Dead End after work.

I got there before him and ordered a tap. I was chewing on peanuts when he came in. He was looking almost as haggard as the professor. He grabbed the stool next to me, caught the bartender's eye, pointed at my beer and held up two fingers. I emptied my glass and slid it towards the other side of the bar. The fresh beers came and Murphy downed half of his in one swallow.

"That bad?" I remarked.

"Yeah," Murphy answered in a monotone. After a moment he looked at me and asked, "So what's this about? Are you trying to pump me for the defense?"

I didn't see any point in denying it. "Maybe. I'm sure Williams would be interested in any new developments. He'll find out anyway from the D. A."

"Well there aren't any."

"Meaning?"

"There's no new evidence linking Hazeltine to the crime. That's what I mean. The prosecutor has been on my case to produce some, but there isn't any. At least not that I've been able to uncover. I've been working overtime the last eight weeks and there's nothing to show for it."

"Maybe there isn't any new evidence because the professor didn't do it." As soon as I said it I knew it was the wrong thing to say. Murphy was obviously frustrated and over worked.

"Don't give me that shit. Do you still believe that your professor is innocent? Who else could have done it? Don't tell me that you're still riding that dead horse about Romanescu?"

"Maybe. Maybe somebody else. What about the boyfriend wanna be? He might have read Hazeltine's book. He was a regular at Hazeltine's afterhours sessions. He was into that kind of stuff. At least enough to stage the scene where Anna's body was found."

"We checked into him. Seeing as we don't know when Anna Smerchek was killed, it'd be hard for him to establish an alibi, but nothing else points to him."

"OK. So it wasn't the boy friend. What makes it so hard for you to believe it was Romanescu?"

Murphy looked at me with a pained expression on his face. "Do you know something that I don't?"

"Yeah. Maybe. I've been checking into Romanescu. Before he came to town he was living in Columbus, Ohio. Ran the same kind of scam, bought an old house, ran an occult bookstore that couldn't possibly have paid the bills."

"We know about that," Murphy protested. "We're not a bunch of amateurs."

"But did you know about the girl they found hanging upside down in an old meat packing plant dressed in a white dress with all her blood drained out?"

Murphy's looked at me with surprise. "When the hell was this?"

"Just before Romanescu sold out and skipped town. Coincidence? Maybe not."

"Fill me in."

I'd kept a copy of the newspaper account tucked into my wallet. I unfolded it, flattened it out on the bar and slid it over towards Murphy. I didn't care if it got wet. I'd made a dozen copies. Murphy looked at it in the light of the fixture hanging over the bar. After a minute he fished inside his jacket for a pair of reading glasses and read it more closely.

"OK. So you found an old crime with similarities to the Smerchek case. That still doesn't tie into Romanescu. Like you said, it just might be a coincidence."

"Just like the similarities between the scene in *The Blood of the Vampyre's Daughter* and Anna Smerchek body."

"OK. Ok. You've made your point. It's still not going to change the D. A.'s mind—" He was going to say more, but his pager interrupted him.

He reached down and turned it off. "Look. I've got to check in. Order another round while I make the call." He walked over to the payphone by the entrance. I got the bartender's attention and ordered a couple of beers. I was tempted to order a couple of shots of rye, but decided to wait. It was just as well. Murphy wasn't long in coming back.

Slamming the beer that the bartender had just brought, he said, "I've got to go. As they say, there've been developments. Hell, pay for the beers. You might as well come along. They've found another body."

I dropped enough money on the bar to cover the tab and followed Murphy out the door.

We drove to an abandoned garage down towards campus. At one time the place had been used by a rock band for practices. They'd painted over all the windows with black paint. There were still a few weathered posters announcing concert dates, but the band, as far as I knew, was long gone, either folded or moved on to bigger and better things.

A police cruiser was out front, it's red lights flashing. Murphy flashed his badge to the officer standing guard, pointed in my direction, and said, "He's with me."

There was a skinny guy, maybe fifty dressed in a shabby navy peacoat, standing next to the cop. He was looking a little green around the gills.

"This is the guy who rents the place. He's the one who called us," the patrolman explained.

"What exactly happened, sir?" Murphy asked in his best polite voice.

"I came to pick something up. I've been using the place to store stuff. Ladder's and things. I'm a painter. Anyway, I went in to get what I wanted. I had a flashlight. The electricity isn't turned on. No point, really. Anyway, I was rummaging around using the flashlight and I saw something in the beam. I went over to check it out. That's when I saw it." It was clear that whatever he'd seen had made an impression.

"What did you see?" Murphy asked gently.

"The body. A dead girl. It was horrible. She was so pale—" At that he choked up.

"That's alright, sir. We'll have to get a statement from you but why don't you go sit in the squad car for a moment. Is it ok for us to go inside? You are the person renting it, aren't you?"

"Yeah. Sure. Go inside if you want."

Murphy was carrying a flashlight from his car. He borrowed another from the patrolman for me.

There was a smaller door next to the big overhead door that had been used to move cars in and out when it was a garage. The smaller door was open. We stepped through. Reflexively Murphy flipped the light switch next to the door up and down, but nothing happened. He turned on his flashlight; so did I. There was a lot of junk, boxes, ladders, empty paint cans scattered near the door, but much of the place was just a big empty room. In the middle there was a table. It looked like it might have been a workbench at one time. Someone had thrown a sheet over it and then laid out the body on top of it. It was a young girl, maybe seventeen though she looked younger. She had long hair and had been dressed in a long white dress. Her hands were folded over her chest just as Anna's had been.

A quick check with a flashlight showed two small puncture wounds on the neck.

"I've seen enough," Murphy said. "What about you?"

I just nodded. We went back outside to wait for the crime lab team.

Murphy went over to the squad car where the painter was sitting, his head between his knees.

"When was the last time you were here? Before tonight, I mean."

"Two weeks ago. I've been out of town. My mother just moved into a new place and I've been helping her fix it up."

"The body wasn't here then?"

"No. Of course not."

"You couldn't have missed it in the dark?"

"I came during the day. I had the big door open to back in my truck because it was raining. There was plenty of light. I couldn't have missed something like that."

"No I don't suppose you could. It's just that it's important to establish when the body was placed there. Do you know of anyone else that's been here since? Did anyone else have a key?"

"No. I don't have any employees. The lock on the door is busted, so I put on a padlock. I've got the only keys."

"That's good to know. Thank you, sir. The officer will take a statement and get your address and then you can go."

We moved off a few feet to wait for the crime lab guys.

"You don't think he did it?" I asked, nodding to the painter.

"Do you?" Murphy said derisively.

"No. But one thing is certain. Hazeltine sure didn't do it. He's been locked up in the jail for the last two months."

"Yeah. I'll give you that."

23.

It turned out that the girl's name was Janice Westbrook, she was seventeen and had run away from a group home in Elgin. She'd had a short and rather unhappy childhood marked by abuse, foster homes and finally petty crime which had landed her in a group home for juvenile offenders. She'd run away from the home two weeks before her body was found. There was no way that Hazeltine could have been involved in her murder.

When that fact came out the newspapers and TV reporters had a field day with it. The same people who days before had been asking for the professor's head on a platter were now railing at the miscarriage of justice that had put an innocent man behind bars and ruined his career. The D. A. took the brunt of the criticism. The police weren't faring much better. The leading paper in town ran a front page story to the effect that the police department had let personal animosity sway them to arrest an innocent man while they let a serial killer run loose. An editorial in the same edition implied that police malfeasance had resulted in Janice Westbrook's death and called for the resignations of the D.A. and the detectives involved. All this ignored the facts that Murphy barely knew Hazeltine and you couldn't really consider a case a serial killer until you had more than one body. Of course, now that was changed.

The D.A. hemmed and hawed and made a statement that "the investigation is ongoing and in light of recent developments the prosecution was reevaluating its position on the case."

Williams made a new motion for dismissal to a judge who was suddenly much more favorably disposed to listen to his plea. The fact that he was facing reelection in the spring may or may not have had something to do with his deliberations on the matter. Three days after the discovery of Janice Westbrook's body, all charges against Professor Hazeltine were dropped and an order for his release from the county jail was issued.

Miss Philips called and asked would it be possible for me to be waiting for the professor when he was released. It seems that there was no one else to handle the chore. Hazeltine might be a free man, but any friends and associates he might have had at the university were conveniently unavailable. As usual, I found it difficult to deny Miss Philips anything. Besides, I felt I owed Hazeltine something after the raw deal he'd gotten.

It might have been late summer, but the day felt more like late fall as I waited in my car outside the gate at the county jail. It was grey and drizzling. I don't think the temperature had broken sixty. I had the heater running to ward off the chill. A couple of guys that I recognized as reporters were also waiting in their cars hoping to catch a quote from the victim of a miscarriage of justice. They worked for the same papers that had printed lurid stories about the professor who performed satanic rituals on coeds.

Hazeltine was supposed to have been released at eleven, but it was closer to noon when he actually appeared at the jailhouse door. He stood for a moment looking up and blinking at the grey sky. He was wearing the same suit he'd had on when they'd arrested him. If anything, he looked more haggard than he had at the conference.

Just before he made his appearance, a camera crew from the local TV station pulled up to record the scene. The reporters who'd been waiting for him got out and jockeyed for position. I got out of my car to run interference for him as he approached the fence. The guard at the gate opened it, and Hazeltine stepped out, finally a free man. The TV reporter stuck a microphone in his face asking for a statement. The professor, tight lipped, looked dazed.

The reporter persisted, and finally pulling himself together, Hazeltine said, "I want to thank my counsel for his work on my behalf and all those friends who have stood by me during this ordeal. Other than that I have no comment at the moment. Thank you." The reporters continued to shout questions, but with a quiet dignity Hazeltine started to walk away.

I muscled my way through and said, "I've got a car waiting." Hazeltine looked at me and just nodded. Still pursued by reporters I walked him over to my car and opened the passenger side door for him. As I slid in the driver's side he said, "Let's get the hell out of here." I started the engine and edged out making it clear I wouldn't object to running over any members of the press that got in my way. In a few moments we'd left them behind.

"Thanks for picking me up. I wasn't sure if there would be anyone waiting. I sure didn't feel like asking the guard to call for a taxi."

"Williams asked me to pick you up. I assume you'll be billed for it."

"Whatever the case, I appreciate it."

"No problem."

"You know what day this is?" Hazeltine asked. He sounded like it was important, but I couldn't figure what he meant by the question.

"No. Not really."

"It's the first day of classes at the university." What he really meant was that he wouldn't be teaching. The university hadn't exactly fired him, but his status was in limbo. Technically, the professor still had tenure, but what was understood was that the university had only been waiting until Hazeltine's conviction to revoke that. The professor's release was certainly going to but a kink in a lot of plans.

I've never understood the whole academic thing, but I understood that being a professor was a big part of who Hazeltine was. Now that whole career was in doubt, possibly wiped out by the D.A.'s political ambitions. I know that being a cop had been a big part of what I was, so much so that when a bullet had put an end to that I'd decided to become a two bit private investigator rather than find a profession that didn't depend on my having two good knees.

Silence hung heavy as we drove away from the county jail.

"That was a nice touch about all the friends that stood by you," I said to make conversation.

"Wasn't it, though. A bunch of rats deserting a sinking ship."

"It was some of your film buddies who put up the money for your defense."

"I'll never speak disparagingly of the film business again," Hazeltine commented wryly. "Unlike those who inhabit the groves of academe. And of course, there's you. You never thought me guilty, did you?"

"No. I guess I didn't."

"Why? If I might ask?"

"You just didn't seem the type. I admit I don't see the fascination in vampires and werewolves and all that stuff. I'm just an simple ex-flatfoot who's a P.I. But I never thought you were nuts. Not in the way this killer is."

"I thank you for that vote of confidence. I mean that sincerely."

"Sure. No problem. Do you want me to take you straight home, or is there something else you want to do?"

"I think I could do with a nice stiff drink," the professor answered. "Possibly a double."

We found a little corner bar. At that hour of the day we had the place to ourselves except for the bartender and an old guy who was doing a crossword puzzle at one end of the bar using a shot and a beer for inspiration. We sat at the other end of the bar so as not to disturb him. The bartender didn't seem either particularly happy or annoyed to see extra customers. The professor ordered a double Johnny Walker. I stuck to beer.

"So what now?" I asked after Hazeltine had taken the first sip of the whisky. He'd shuddered a little, but a smile had broken his face for the first time since I'd met him at the jail gate.

"I really don't know. Until yesterday I didn't have a future. Now, I'm a free man, but what does that mean? Can my life go back to what it was? I doubt it. I'm not even sure that I have a job at the university anymore."

"Sorry about that."

"It wasn't your fault. You were one of the few people that didn't think I was some kind of monster. Thanks again." He raised his glass to me and then took another sip.

"Don't mention it," I said staring at our reflections in the mirror behind the bar. After a moment I said, "This thing has made a mess of a lot of lives. Vern Smerchek called me the other night. It looks like he and his wife are separating. I'm not sure what's going to happen with Anna's sister. Murphy is taking it hard, too, though I suppose that doesn't bother you."

"All collateral damage. You never think about that when you read about something like this happening, but there are always more victims than just the dead. What about you? How are you holding up?"

I looked at the professor. He seemed genuinely concerned. "Me? Oh I'll get by. I just don't know if I'll ever forget the sight of those two girls laid out like that."

"You know it was all a game to me; vampires, werewolves, the whole weird spectrum. None of it was supposed to be real. Just ghost stories told around a campfire for entertainment while marshmallows roasted on spits. No one was supposed to ever die. I'm not sure I can deal with that stuff again."

"Nothing you did caused those girl's death, professor. If the girl in Ohio is part of it, too, it started a long time ago in another place."

The professor shook his head and took a long sip of his Scotch.

"Are they any closer to catching whoever killed them?"

"Not so far as I can tell. So far, Romanescu is still just a half-baked theory. There's no solid evidence pinning him to either crime."

"But you think he's the one, don't you?"

"Yeah. I do."

After that we had another drink, then I drove the professor home. We stopped to pick up Chinese on the way for his dinner.

24.

It seemed that the professor still had some friends at the university after all. Either that or guilt at abandoning him was producing feelings of remorse. Whatever the reason, they decided to throw a "welcome home" party for Hazeltine a few days after his release.

By then, the professor was getting back some of his spirit. Things were looking up for him. Whether from a sense of fair play or the threat of a lawsuit from Waldorf, Williams, and Wohlberg, the university had agreed to reinstate him for the fall semester. A few seminars and honors classes were hastily arranged to justify paying him a salary for the term and he'd resume his normal schedule for the spring term. When Hazeltine called me to invite me to the party he had seemed almost happy.

As parties go, it wasn't much. They held it in the small banquet room of an Italian restaurant near the campus. There was an open bar of sorts that consisted of a keg of beer and a few bottles of cheap Chianti. Stronger stuff was available on a cash basis at the restaurant's bar. There was a buffet that consisted mostly of cocktail weenies, meat balls, and garlic bread. Besides the professor and myself only a dozen or so people showed up, mostly faculty from the English and drama departments and a few grad students who seemed more interested in the free beer and weenies than the professor. A few of the students I recognized from the afterhours session I'd gone to at the start of things. That seemed such a long time ago.

Things were in full swing when I got there, by which I mean people were standing around in clumps holding drinks in one hand and paper plates with meat balls in the other. The professor was standing talking to a woman about his age holding a nearly empty glass of wine. The professor had equipped himself with a large scotch. He seemed relieved to see me.

"This is Hilda Weinberg. She's in the drama department," Hazeltine said by way of introduction. "Hilda, this is the private eye that stood by me through thick and thin." The professors sounded a little drunk. I couldn't say that I blamed him.

"Charmed," Weinberg said, extending a hand after awkwardly shifting her wine glass to the hand holding the paper plate. "We're so glad that George has been exonerated. He's too much of an original voice for the university to lose."

Hazeltine seemed embarrassed by the sentiment. So did Weinberg for that matter. She left a moment later in search of more Chianti. The professor and I exchanged a few pleasantries before I went to get a glass of beer. I grabbed a couple of meatballs and a slice of garlic bread, too. I hadn't had any dinner and lunch was just a memory.

When I returned, Hazeltine was standing in the middle of the room alone. It appeared that with the exception of Ms. Weinberg, his colleagues were willing to welcome him back to academe, they just didn't want to be seen talking to him.

"Pretty lame, isn't it?" Hazeltine said.

"Give it time, professor."

"Easy for you to say."

"Look, the same sort of thing happened to me when I came back after I was shot. Everybody was all happy to see me as long as they didn't have to get too close. It was like it my gunshot was contagious."

"And how did that turn out for you?"

"Point taken." I'd been granted disability pay and forcibly retired. People had promised to stay in touch, but they never did. The break had become complete when I got my investigator's license.

We stood around, trying to make small talk. Gradually the crowd started to thin out. A bus boy came to remove the hot dishes holding the remaining meatballs and weenies. Ms. Weinberg tried to pour the last drops of Chianti into her empty glass, and then gave a shrug and headed for the ladies room.

"My glass is empty," Hazeltine said. "Do you want to head to the bar for something stronger?"

"Sure, why not?" I got the impression that the professor wanted to talk.

The professor ordered a double scotch on the rocks. I'm normally a rye man, but I followed suit. I wouldn't let Hazeltine pay. Whatever his ordeal had been for him, it had been a bonanza for me. I'd billed Waldorf, Williams, and Wohlberg for twice my normal monthly hours on the case.

I was about to toast the professor when I caught a funny look in his eye. He was staring towards the entrance.

"What the hell is he doing here?" Hazeltine asked in a tone caught between fear and anger.

I turned to see Murphy standing in the doorway scanning the room. If anything, he was looking even more tired and haggard than he had when we'd found Janice Westbrook.

I looked back at the professor trying to gauge his reaction to see if I'd have to get between the two, but Hazeltine was just gripping his glass and staring at the back bar. I was hoping that Murphy was there for some other reason, but it was obvious he'd come looking for us because he walked up to where we were sitting.

"If you came to crash the party, you're a little late," Hazeltine remarked bitterly. "Or are you here to arrest me again?"

I could see a flash of anger in the detective's eyes, but it cooled quickly. "I guess maybe I deserved that. Look, I don't want to hassle you, I just came to tell you that I'm sorry."

I had to hand it to Murphy. Not every man is big enough to admit it when he's been wrong. The question was how was Hazeltine going to take it.

I guess I shouldn't have been worried. He turned to face Murphy and said, "I guess you were just doing what you thought was your job."

"It's just that I really thought you were guilty, and by the time I started to have my doubts the D.A. had gotten his teeth into the case and was seeing the headlines—"

"As an apology, this leaves a lot to be desired," Hazeltine said sarcastically.

"Yeah. I guess this wasn't such a hot idea. Well I said my piece. I'll be going."

"Oh, what the hell," the professor said. "Take a seat and have a drink with us. What's done is done and can't be undone."

Murphy looked like he was going to refuse for a moment and then just slumped onto the stool next to me. When the bartender came over he ordered a shot of Jameson's, which just goes to prove the old saying, "you can take the cop out of Ireland but you can't take the Irish out of the cop."

He raised the shot glass in salute and then downed it in one long sip. I was beginning to wonder what demons Murphy was trying to exorcise.

"Let me buy the next round," Murphy said as he slammed the glass on the bar. Hazeltine and I still had half full glasses, but it occurred to me that maybe what the professor needed was a good drunk. Murphy got the bartender's attention and gestured for refills for the three of us. I hadn't had anything to eat except a couple of meatballs and three cocktail weenies, but I decided that didn't matter.

"So what's eating you, Murphy?" I asked after the bartender had deposited the three glasses on the bar.

Murphy took a sip of his drink before answering, then said, "This business is over now for you two. Me, I've still got a crazy killer to catch, and I don't have a clue how to find him."

"There's still Romanescu," I reminded him.

"You keep bringing him up, but where's your proof? Or even anything to tie him to the case?"

"You got anyone better in mind?"

"No," Murphy answered reluctantly. "That's the problem. What I need is some fresh ideas. Professor, who do you think killed those girls?"

"That's really not my line of work," Hazeltine replied. "What you need is someone who specializes in abnormal psychology."

"Maybe, professor, but what I've got at the moment is you. I'd really like to know what you think."

"OK. I think we can agree that the murderer is nuts," Hazeltine said, sounding like, well he was sounding like a college professor giving a lecture. "But he's nuts in a very particular way. From what I've read about them, the murders weren't sadistic.

They weren't even particularly violent. But they were very ritualistic in nature, and that implies some sort of belief in what he's doing. These girls were killed for a purpose."

"What kind of purpose requires draining the blood from the body?" Murphy asked.

"That's a good question, and when you have the answer you'll probably have your man. My whole point is that for the murderer, killing in this particular manner is an attempt to achieve some goal."

"Which would be?"

"I don't know. Power, health, immortality—"

"Immortality?"

"Think about it. It's the blood. It wasn't splashed around in some killing frenzy. It was collected, neatly, precisely. Why? Because the killer planned to do something with it."

"I don't follow you professor. What did he do with the blood?"

"I don't know," Hazeltine responded. He was warming up to the subject. "What can you do with blood? You can drink it, bathe in it, use it as an ingredient in some magic potion, pour it on your Wheaties in the morning. But for the killer, the blood, the blood of a young virgin, has some sort of potency, some mystical power."

"You make him sound like one of your vampires, professor," Murphy said.

"Precisely. The killer is acting just like a vampire."

"You can't sit there and tell me with a straight face that you actually believe in vampires, professor, can you?"

"It's not what I believe. It's what the killer believes that is important. And if you ask me, he thinks he is a vampire. Or maybe it's just that he wants to become a vampire, and that's the reason for killings."

"But why keep killing?"

"Because so far the ritual has failed him. He hasn't yet become a real vampire, so he must keep trying until he succeeds. In his mind it's a question of refining the ritual until he gets it right. The killing in Columbus was rather crude. He hung up his victim and treated it like an animal carcass. Anna Smerchek's killing was much more sophisticated, as if the killer was trying to correct the mistakes he'd made in the previous attempt. He seems to have drawn some inspiration from *The Blood of the Vampyre's Daughter* and my book. For all we know, the process of this latest murder, the Westbrook girl, was even more refined."

"So this guy is just going to keep killing?"

"Until he gets it right," the professor said. "Except that unless there really are such things as vampires he's never going to get it right. He'll just keep on killing until he's caught."

"So how am I supposed to catch this guy?"

"By thinking like he does. By thinking like a vampire."

"Just how am I supposed to do that?" Murphy asked in disgust.

"Read my book. It appears the killer has."

"Why should I bother to read the book when I've got the author right at hand?"

"Now just a minute—" Hazeltine protested.

It would have been interesting to see where that conversation was headed but at that moment the bartender was shouting, "Is there a Detective Sergeant Murphy here? There's a phone call."

"Here," Murphy shouted back.

The bartender brought the phone over. There was a short conversation that consisted mostly of "Uh-huhs" on Murphy's part. "What's the address?" The detective wrote something down in his notebook. "I'll be right there."

"I've got to go. There's been another one."

"Sorry to hear that," Hazeltine said.

"Yeah. You know, maybe it's time to put your theory to the test, Professor. Why don't you and the shamus here come along and see if you can give me some insight into this killer?"

ROMANESCU

25.

It turned out that her name really was Coleen Smith. Of course, we didn't know that at the time. She was also the salesgirl from the bookstore at the House of Esoteric Wisdom.

Hazeltine and I rode in the back seat of Murphy's car, some police regulation or other. Neither one of us said anything, just letting the policeman drive. I'm not sure that either one of us really wanted to be there, but we both knew that we were caught up in something and had to see it through.

I can't say I was surprised when Murphy turned into the grounds of "The Garden of Rest," the oldest cemetery in town. Hazeltine gave me a questioning look, but I just responded with a shrug. I'd no more idea where we were going than he did. Murphy seemed to know where he was going, and he was the one driving.

As we followed one of the winding lanes that ran through the cemetery, it became pretty obvious where we were going. There was already a police cruiser with its flashing lights on parked to the side of the lane, a white faced police woman standing besides it. Murphy pulled up behind her and we got out.

She seemed to know Murphy, so there were no introductions. She nodded towards the professor and me, but Murphy just responded with a terse "They're with me."

"The body is up there in the mausoleum," the policewoman said, pointing to a crypt that stood at the summit of a low hill. "One of the grounds keepers noticed that the door to the crypt wasn't shut all the way. Normally it's kept locked. He went to investigate and found the body. He went back to the office and called dispatch. They sent me."

She didn't seem to have anything to add, so Murphy started walking towards the crypt. Hazeltine and I fell in behind.

The mausoleum was like something you don't expect to see outside of a horror movie. It was a low, stone building, half sunk into the hillside, not particularly big, maybe ten by sixteen feet. From the ornate neo-classical details covering the stone facade it was obvious that it had been designed with Victorian sensibilities in mind. A short set of steps led downwards towards the entrance like a portal into the underworld. A family name that I recognized as having been locally prominent in the last century was carved into the marble above the doorway.

Murphy had grabbed a flashlight when we'd gotten out of his car. With it firmly in hand he went down the steps, not so much with trepidation as resignation. The patrol officer had left the door open, so he stood on the threshold and shone the beam of the flashlight into the crypt.

He stood there a long time swinging the beam of the flashlight into one corner and then another. Finally he said, "You can come down, but don't touch anything. Remember, this is a crime scene." Then he entered the mausoleum.

I followed, Hazeltine coming after me.

It seemed smaller inside than it had from above, but given the nature of the construction, that was to be expected. The two side walls were lined with niches, four high. Coffins had been slid into the lower ones, but several of the top spaces were empty. Evidently, the family had died out before the crypt had filled up. In the center was a stone sarcophagus, presumably the resting place of the family patriarch. It was on top of this that the body had been laid out.

The presentation was familiar. The corpse wearing a long white dress, lying on its back with hands draped chastely over the breasts. For our benefit, Murphy pointed the flashlight to the side of the neck so that we could see the two small red puncture marks.

"Recognize her?" Murphy asked, shining the flash on her face.

I stared at the face for a moment before it clicked. Sometime in the last few months she had died her hair black, but it was still long and straight. Her body was still rail thin. It was the girl from Romanescu's bookstore.

I glanced at the professor to see his reaction. He was looking a little green around the gills, but there wasn't a hint of recognition in his eyes.

After a moment he said, "If you gentlemen will excuse me, I think I need a breath of fresh air." I can't say that I blamed him. Besides, he had seen enough to get the idea.

"Still doubt that Romanescu is involved?" I asked.

"Maybe. Maybe it's just a coincidence," Murphy replied.

"Come off it. You can't tell me you really believe that."

"It doesn't matter what I believe. I need evidence. I went with my gut with your professor friend and look where that got me. I'm not going to make the same mistake again on this case."

I let it rest. Murphy had already made his act of contrition towards Hazeltine which is more than many men would have done.

"Let's get out of here," Murphy said finally. "We can't do anything until forensics and the M.E. have done their jobs."

I didn't protest.

Topside, Hazeltine looked a little better. Not great, but better. The crime lab people had shown up and were getting their gear organized. We moved off to the side to be out of the way.

"Were the other two girls found like this?" the professor asked.

"More or less," Murphy answered.

"I can see why you were suspicious. It does bear an uncanny resemblance to the scene in '*The Blood of the Vampyre's Daughter*.' Not that many people actually saw the movie."

"He might have read your book," Murphy commented.

"Are we so sure it was a man that did this?" I asked just to keep in the conversation.

"Oh, I think we can safely assume it was a man," Hazeltine replied. "I'm no expert on psychology, but there is definitely a sexual element to the murderer's actions."

"Neither of the other two had been sexually molested in any way. In fact, both were virgins."

"Not surprising.   Throughout history virginity has been endowed with a certain mystical power. But when I said that I thought there was a sexual element, I wasn't referring to anything as crude as rape. In the killer's mind this is all about power. He is trying to enhance his own personal force by ritualistically drawing from another's. He achieves this through the drinking of the blood of his victims, but in his eyes, it's really a form of marriage, hence his preying on the opposite sex."

"You don't really believe in all that stuff, do you professor?" Murphy asked derisively.

"It doesn't matter what I believe, Sergeant. It's what the killer believes, and I think we have to assume that he believes that he is a vampire, or if not that, that he is trying to become one. And why not? Immortal life, great strength, power to control other people, those are all powerful motivations you'll have to agree."

"All I care about is catching him before he does this to someone else."

"Of course," Hazeltine agreed.

"There was one difference," I said. "From the first two girls, I mean."

"What was that? It looked pretty much the same to me."

"Did you look at her wrists? Or her feet?" I asked

"What do you mean?"

"Both Anna and the other girl had marks showing that they had been bound before they died. I didn't see that on this girl."

"What about it?" Murphy asked.

"It meant that she was a willing participant in the ritual. Whoever did this convinced her to lie there while he bled her out."

"You can't mean that. Who would just lie there while they were being killed?"

"Maybe she didn't think she was going to die," Hazeltine said.

"That's nuts."

"We aren't dealing with rational thought, Sergeant. We're talking about faith and belief. The anthropological record is full of examples of people willingly submitting to all sorts of tortures because they believe in something."

"But what could she expect would happen?"

"Why, I would have thought it to be obvious. She expected to become a vampire just like her mentor."

For no particularly good reason we hung around while the forensics team and the M.E. went about their business. There really wasn't anything we could do, and the lab people wouldn't have most of the results for days. Still, we didn't leave.

Dr. Morton was the man from the Medical Examiner's office. When he emerged from the crypt he saw Murphy and came over.

"In answer to your questions, even though you haven't asked them yet, yes, all the blood has been drained from her body, and I can't be sure yet, but a rough measurement indicates that the same instrument was probably used to drain the blood as in the other two cases. Other than the two puncture wounds, there are no visible signs of trauma, but I only examined those parts of the body that were visible outside her clothing. The rest will have to wait till the autopsy. I'm assuming that there will be one. It seems likely. I'll do a full toxicological screen, of course, but it will probably be days before I have the results back. It will be harder because we have to run the tests on tissue rather than blood. There is no blood."

"Thanks doc. Let me know if anything useful shows up."

"Of course. I need to get going. My wife is holding dinner for me." The doctor headed for his car.

"I guess there's no point hanging around here," Murphy said. "I don't know about you two, but I could use a drink."

26.

We found a quiet bar nearby. The only other people in the place besides the bartender were a couple nursing beers at the end of the bar. They looked like neighborhood regulars in for a nightcap after dinner. The bartender didn't seemed all that pleased to have more customers. I got the impression that all he really wanted was to close up and go home.

I ordered a scotch and soda. So did the professor. Murphy gazed at the bottles behind the bar, thought better of it and ordered a tap. He'd been drinking pretty hard earlier, but he knew his limits.

"So what now?" Murphy asked.

"What do you mean?"

"How do we catch this guy? What else?"

"You admit it's Romanescu, then?"

"I'm willing to accept that he's a suspect. OK, maybe the prime suspect. But how do I get proof?"

"Search his place. You should have grounds for a warrant now."

"Do I? You and I recognized her as working in his bookstore, but will that convince a judge? I'm not so sure, especially since we've looked the place over once already."

"Whatever we do, we should do it fast before Romanescu has a chance to clean up the evidence."

"I'm not so sure the girls were killed at the house. I think he's got some other place where he conducts his sacrifices."

Hazeltine had been quiet up to this point, but now he chimed in: "I think the sergeant is right. Whoever did this didn't just incapacitate his victims and bleed them to death like he was bleeding a pig. There was a ritual involved, almost like a mass. The ritual probably requires props—"

"What kind of props?" Murphy interrupted, suddenly attentive.

"I don't know. Candles, probably materials to create a pentagram, a basin of some sort to collect the blood, maybe a ritual dagger. Things like that."

"So where do you get that kind of stuff?"

"Mail order. Probably the same suppliers that he used for the bookstore assuming that it is Romanescu."

"More grounds for a warrant to check his books," I added.

"And about the place where he's doing this. I think it has to be a special place. A place of power."

"A place of power? What's that supposed to mean?" Murphy asked.

"Someplace with some sort of sacred history. Someplace where other types of rituals have been performed in the past. Someplace such as a formerly consecrated church or chapel."

"What makes you think that?" Murphy asked.

"Think about it. The three victims were laid out at a location other than where they were killed, essentially someplace where the killer thought they wouldn't be discovered right away, an abandoned house, what he thought was an unused garage, an old crypt. All just convenient places where he could lay out the bodies after the ritual. But why didn't he perform the ritual in those places? Because he needs a special sort of place, that's why. And why not leave them where he killed them? Because he doesn't want that special place discovered. It's a place for which he might not easily be able to find a replacement. That's why he moves the bodies."

"When you explain it like that it almost makes sense, Professor."

Murphy stood there leaning on the bar. I could see the wheels going around in his head. Finally he asked, "Are you in, Professor?"

"What do you mean?"

"Are you willing to help me catch this guy?"

"A few days ago you had me locked up because you thought I was the killer. Now you want me to help you?"

"Yeah. I'm out of my depth with this case. I admit it. You seem to have some idea of what this guy is up to. I don't, and I'm going to need all the help I can get."

"You've got a lot of nerve, sergeant," Hazeltine said.

"Yeah. I've been told that," Murphy replied.

Hazeltine looked away for a moment. Then he said, "I'll think about it. Right now, it's late, I'm tired, and I've had too much to drink. I just want to go home. Should I call a cab?"

"No. You're right, Professor. It is late, and I've got a lot to do in the morning. I'll see you home."

The M.E. didn't have much trouble identifying the latest victim. It turned out she'd been arrested for petty theft a few years previous and her prints were on file. Her name was Coleen Smith and she would have been twenty-one in December. Murphy told me this when he called saying he'd got a warrant to search the House of Esoteric Wisdom. He wanted me to come along and bring Hazeltine.

I wasn't sure the professor would be up for it, but to my surprise he agreed eagerly. I said that I'd pick him up.

Murphy had arranged for a couple of patrol cars with uniforms in addition to a pair of homicide detectives. He sent one of the patrolmen around the back and put the other one where he could watch both sides of the building. The professor and I were to wait outside until he gave the word.

The place seemed to be closed up. The front door was locked and no one responded when Murphy knocked. The detectives drew their guns. Murphy pounded on the door louder and announced that it was the police, but there wasn't any response. Finally he grabbed the door handle and put his shoulder to it. That wouldn't have worked for me, but Murphy is a beefy guy. There was a crack and the door swung open.

The three detectives disappeared inside. It seemed like forever, but it was probably only five minutes later when Murphy came out onto the porch and motioned for us to join him.

"I take it no one is home?" I asked.

"Yeah. It looks like Romanescu has flown the coop. No one else was here. It looks like Romanesu and a woman, probably the latest victim, were living upstairs. Separate bedrooms. Women's clothes in one, no clothing left in the other bedroom. Looks like Romanescu had time to pack a bag before leaving. There's some food left in the refrigerator in the kitchen, including a half-gallon of milk that hasn't spoiled."

"Any signs of—well you know?" I asked.

"No. The basement is pretty much empty. I'll have the lab boys go over it, but my guess is it's clean. Seems you were right, Professor, if Romanescu is our killer, he's doing his work somewhere else."

"Is there anything you want us to do, sergeant?" Hazeltine asked.

"You can look over the place, see if you spot anything. There's lots of weird books around the place. Probably mostly junk, but you might recognize something in them. One of my men is going over the bookstore seeing if he can find the account books. I'll let you know if I need you to look at those."

Murphy and the other detectives seemed to be concentrating on the downstairs so I steered the professor to the top floor. This was laid out in a pretty conventional manner, two bedrooms towards the front, a bath and another bedroom to the back. The two front bedrooms were empty except for mattresses laying on the floor. Evidently they were reserved for the occasional drop-ins that Romanescu offered a place for the night.

It was apparent that the bedroom in the rear had been used by Coleen Smith. It was furnished with a single bed against one wall, a cheap dresser, and a chair that looked like they had been bought at St. Vincent's. There was a small closet in which some of her clothes still hung, mostly dresses in black. The dresser revealed a modest supply of underwear, some t-shirts and sweaters.

A purse stood open on the top of the dresser. It didn't contain much, a hair-brush, a key chain with a couple of what looked like house-keys on it and a wallet. The wallet was empty of cash, but it did hold a driver's license and a library card. When

I saw the library card the association came back to me in a rush, the place that I'd seen Coleen Smith's name before. She'd been the one that had checked out Hazeltine's book, *Vampyres – Fact and Fiction*.

While I'd been going through the dresser, Hazeltine had picked up a book from the nightstand next to the bed and was leafing through it intently.

"Anything interesting?"

"It's a book by Aleister Crowley," the professor said as if that should have meant something.

"Is that important?"

"Crowley was a figure in the first half of the century. He wrote extensively on magic, by which I mean the real thing, not stage illusions. Mostly it's a load of crap, but he's pretty influential amongst those that believe in black magic."

"So a little light bed-time reading?" I commented.

"For some."

"Have you read any of his stuff?" I asked out of curiosity.

"I've tried a couple of times. Like I said it's mostly junk. Mostly theories that he made up to suit his personal philosophy. Still, there's more to it than most books on the occult."

"So this Coleen Smith believed in black magic?"

"Or wanted to believe. From what you and the sergeant have said, this Romanescu sounds like he was the sort that liked to manipulate the minds of his followers and he had the personality to carry it off."

"Enough so that this girl would let him drain the blood from her?"

"Maybe," Hazeltine answered. "Though I wouldn't be surprised if he also employed drugs to make his victims more pliable."

"Nice guy."

"Nice guys don't drain the blood from their dates," Hazeltine commented.

"Find anything else interesting?"

"No. It looks as if she lived a pretty pathetic sort of life."

"Yeah. From the outside it looks like somebody was living in the attic. Probably Romanescu. Let's check it out if you're done here."

"Fine by me." He placed the book back on the nightstand where he'd found it.

The attic room had obviously been Romanescu's. Whereas the lower floors had been sparsely furnished, the attic had been done over in a kind of second hand luxury. There was a double bed, an old but comfortable looking arm-chair flanked by a floor lamp and side table. A worn Persian carpet covered the floorboards in the center of the room and various pieces of fabric were hung from the rafters like tapestries. The affect was much like that of the tent of some desert potentate. It was clear who had sat at the top of the hierarchy of the House of Esoteric Wisdom.

The professor and I poked around the attic for awhile, but there wasn't much to find other than a few old books. Hazeltine looked at these briefly, but there was nothing that caught his attention. Romanescu might have been forced to leave his furniture, but he had cleared out any personal effects. It was obvious that he wasn't planning to return. We headed back downstairs.

Murphy was pacing the entry hall, clearly discouraged.

"Did you find anything?" he asked curtly.

"Not much. You might find out if Coleen Smith owned a car. There was a set of keys in her purse to a Volkswagen. I also found her library card."

"So she read. What's the big deal?"

"She was the last one to check out Hazeltine's book from the library, the one that seems to have been the inspiration for the staging of the bodies."

"Did you find the book?" Murphy said attentively.

"No. The girl was reading a book on black magic, though."

"Great. It's bad enough to have a guy who thinks he's a vampire. Now I've got someone trying to learn to be a witch."

"She's dead," I reminded him.

"Yeah," Murphy replied, sounding tired again. "We've looked through the stuff in the bookstore, Professor, but we couldn't make head or tails of it. Care to take a look?"

Hazeltine had been subdued. I think the realization that we were in a place associated with the death of three young women was getting to him. Murphy's request gave him something to occupy his mind.

I followed him into the room that had served as the bookstore. He glanced at the stuff in the glass case and the front window and dismissed their contents. He paid a little more attention to the bookshelves behind the counter, pulling out certain volumes, opening them and then shoving them back into place. It was a glass fronted bookcase in the corner that got his attention. He tried the door, but it seemed to be locked. Failing to open it, he tried to read the titles through the dusty glass.

"Any way we can get this open? Most of the rest of this stuff is junk, the kind of thing you can pick up in any head shop or occult bookstore in the country, but I think the stuff in this cabinet may be more interesting."

Murphy, who had trailed us into the bookstore went over to the cabinet. When the door failed to open he brought out a pocket knife and stuck the blade in the crack by the lock. There was a sudden snap of wood and the door swung open.

"It's all yours, Professor."

Hazeltine bent over close to peer at the contents. Seemingly at random, he pulled a few of the books out and opened them. The books were old, and by that I mean not just a few decades, but a century or more. From what I could see glancing over the professor's shoulder most of them weren't in English. Some were in Latin and others used that gothic sort of typeface you see in old German books. I wasn't sure about the language of the rest. At least a few were written in Hebrew.

"These are the real deal," Hazeltine said softly, almost reverently.

"What do you mean by that, Professor?" Murphy asked.

"I mean they're old. Eighteenth, nineteenth century. Some earlier. My Latin is a little rusty. So is my German for that matter, but the ones that I can read are all on occult subjects, vampires, werewolves, that kind of things, but they're the original accounts, not later commentaries, and they're the first editions, not later reprints. Whoever gathered these was serious about the subject. By that I mean it would have cost a lot of money to collect these. Some of these aren't even supposed to exist anymore."

"Don't get too excited, Professor. Remember, they're evidence."

"Of course. But if there's any way these could end with the university—"

"We'll see how things turn out. Maybe Romanescu will come back to claim them. I'd like that. You say these are the real deal. You don't really believe in what's in them."

"No," Hazeltine said shaking his head, "but the people who wrote them believed it. That's what makes them so fascinating."

"OK. Fascinating stuff. Historical. I understand that. But what do they tell us about this Romanescu guy? Is he the killer? Can they help us find him?"

"I think they confirm the fact that he's not just some drugged out hippy who's had a bad acid trip. He's probably been seriously delusional for a long time. It would have taken years to amass this collection. Years and a lot of money. He wouldn't have done that just because he found them interesting. He's had to have thought that he'd find what he was looking for somewhere in these books."

"And what was that?" I asked.

"What we've been talking about. He wants to become a vampire. Or an immortal, or whatever, but something that transcends mere humanity."

"OK. So if these books were so important to him, why'd he leave them behind?"

"Maybe he was in a hurry. Maybe he thinks he already knows the answers to the questions he's been asking."

"What do you mean by that, Professor?" Murphy asked quietly, like Hazeltine's answer was suddenly important.

"I mean he thinks he knows what went wrong with his previous attempts to become a vampire. And that means we can expect him to try again. Probably soon."

"You mean he's going to kill again?" Murphy asked.

"Yes. Why wouldn't he? The only reason he wouldn't try again is if he'd actually succeeded."

"Succeeded?"

"Yes. Succeeded in becoming a vampire."

"You're creeping me out, Professor. You don't really mean that."

"Of course not," Hazeltine answered soberly. "But the only way Romanescu is going to stop of his own accord is if he thinks he's succeeded. But we both know that isn't possible, don't we."

27.

As you can imagine, after the third body was found, the news media went crazy. They'd been riding the story for half a year since it had first broke. After the discovery of Anna Smerchek's body they had been after Hazeltine's head, convinced that the professor was a monster preying on the young women of the city. When Janice Westbrook was discovered proving the professor's innocence, they had railed at the miscarriage of justice that had put an innocent man in jail. But with the third body, a note of fear had crept into the musings of the press. The story was no longer about the incompetence of the police or the depravity of a faculty member. It was now openly acknowledged that there was a serial killer on the loose, an elusive night monster threatening the lives of any member of the fairer sex from five to ninety-five.

Up to that point, the police had managed to keep a lid on the more grizzly aspects of the murders, only referring vaguely to certain "ritualistic elements" at the scenes where the bodies had been discovered. Somehow, though, details started to leak out, whether from within the police department or the medical examiner's office, or from someone more peripherally involved with the case. Once the press got hold of the information that the victims had been drained of their blood and of the two puncture wounds to the neck, they went crazy. The front pages of the local papers carried stories of the "blood-sucking demon" terrorizing the city. Even the national press started to chime in with reports, christening Romanescu the "Vampire Killer."

Hazeltine was asked to write an article for one of the papers giving background information on the vampire legend throughout history. Wisely, he declined as he did with a request for a television interview. Neither refusal deterred the press who went ahead with articles quoting liberally from *Vampyres – Fact and Fiction* and citing the professor as the world renowned expert on the subject.

Needless to say, the pressure on the police, the D.A.s office, the mayor and every other branch of local government to end the "vampire menace" was enormous. The morning paper called for the mayor to resign, the evening journal carried an editorial calling on the mayor to fire the police chief. One TV station called on the governor to mobilize the National Guard.

Rumor and misinformation were rampant. Panic gripped the city. The streets were deserted after dark and people left their porch-lights on throughout the night. Even the bars reported a downturn in their evening business. Despite the best efforts of the city's grocers, garlic was in short supply.

It was in this atmosphere that Murphy called a council of war. Despite only being a detective sergeant, he had been put in command of the task force charged with the capture of Romanescu. The cynic in me suspected the choice had been made so that none of the department's higher-ups would be implicated if the effort should fail. Hazeltine and I had been appointed as "civilian consultants" to the task force. It didn't escape my notice that I wasn't getting paid for my participation.

Murphy had commandeered one of the conference rooms in the court house as a war room. A map of the city had been stuck up on the wall with different colored push pins depicting points of interest, red for the sites where the bodies had been found, blue for the House of Esoteric Wisdom and the vacant lot Coleen Smith had given as her address when applying for her library card, green for the dormitory where Anna Smerchek had lived, etc. A bulletin board contained pictures of the murdered girls, though the only photos of Coleen Smith were the one from the crypt where she had been found and a dated one from her shoplifting arrest. There were also several stills from *Blood of the Vampyre's Daughter*. There were no photos of Romanescu. One of the patrolmen assigned to the task force asked Hazeltine seriously if that was because vampires can't be photographed. His reply that that was only true if the camera used mirrors was not appreciated by Murphy.

When everyone involved had been assembled, Murphy got up in front to address them. He was looking ever more haggard.

I knew from his remarks that he wasn't getting much in the way of sleep. Not that any of us were.

"OK. I've called you all together so that we can go over what we know about this case so far, so that we can brainstorm and maybe come up with a plan to catch this guy before he kills again. I assume those of you who are cops know each other. This is Dr. Morton from the medical examiner's office," Murphy said, indicating the pathologist. "He's the one who did the autopsies. This gentleman is Professor Hazeltine. He's here, and I want to stress this, not because he is an expert on vampires, because there are no such things, but because he is an expert about what people think about vampires. We have reason to believe that Romanescu has been influenced by one of the professor's books and by a movie that he worked on, *Blood of the Vampyre's Daughter*." He introduced me simply as a private investigator that had worked for Anna Smerchek's family.

Murphy gave a short history of the case, starting with the disappearance of Anna Smerchek, and ending with the search of the House of Esoteric Wisdom. Dr. Morton gave a short précis of the post mortem's he'd performed on the three girls. Photos of the crime scenes where the bodies had been found were passed around and mention was made about the resemblance to the scene in *Vampyre's Daughter*. There were a few sideways glances at Hazeltine.

"Look, I didn't have anything to do with that scene," he protested. "It was the idea of one of the screenwriters." I don't know if his denial did any good.

Murphy called the meeting back to attention. "That's what we know for sure, and it's not much. There are some things that are more speculative. In Columbus, Ohio, where Romanescu lived for five years before coming here there was a murder of a another young girl that shares some similarities with this case, but other than the fact that he was in Columbus at the time, there is nothing specific to tie Romanescu to that crime."

"What were the similarities?" one of the detectives asked.

"All the blood had been drained out of the victim," Murphy said.

"She'd been hung upside down from a meat hook in an old meat packing plant and bled like a hog," I added. "There was no staging of the body afterward, and the wound to the neck was different.   The theory is that it was a first attempt on Romanescu's part and he was still working on technique. Draw your own conclusions."

"How sure are we that it's this Romanescu guy?" another detective asked. He was an older guy, maybe a year short of retirement. I knew him slightly from when I'd been on the force, he was a no nonsense kind of old school cop.

"Good question, Ed," Murphy said. "We know that the last victim worked for Romanescu in his bookshop. She also lived in the same house. We know that Anna Smerchek, the first victim, visited the House of Esoteric Wisdom on at least one occasion to hear Romanescu lecture. We have reason to suspect that she returned, but no hard evidence.   The second girl, Janice Westbrook, was a runaway. Romanescu is known to have let people sleep at his place, but we have no evidence that this was the case with the Westbrook girl.   Everything else is circumstantial, but Romanescu did disappear immediately after Coleen Smith was killed. As our P.I. friend here said, draw your own conclusions."

"Any reason to think he's still in town?"

"Romanescu didn't own a car or have a driver's license. Coleen Smith did own a V.W. which she kept in a garage behind the House of Esoteric Wisdom. It was found abandoned a few miles away two days after her body was found. There were no useable prints from anyone besides the owner. None of the bus companies or airlines remember a passenger fitting Romanescu's description."

"What about his past?" I asked.

"We don't know anything about the time before Columbus, except that he came there from out east somewhere. We think that he was originally from Europe, but the accent may be a phony."

"Have you had any more luck with the State Department than I did?"

"Not much. They confirmed that someone named Vladimir Romanescu was given assistance after the collapse of the Hungarian revolt in 1956. He was allowed to enter this country and given refugee status. Unfortunately, at least according to the State Department, they lost touch with him shortly after he arrived. They didn't say so in so many words, but the impression they gave that was that Romanescu had been working with the CIA."

"Great," one of the patrolmen said, "Not only is he a vampire but he's a spook, as well."

"Can it," Murphy said.

"Sergeant," Hazeltine said quietly. "How old was this Romanescu of the State Department's?"

"The copy of the entry visa they sent me said he was about thirty. It didn't have an exact birth date. Not that uncommon. Lots of records were destroyed during the war."

"Yes, but that was back in 1956. That's almost twenty years ago, which would make him around fifty. You've seen Romanescu. How old did he look?"

"I don't know. It's hard to tell with a guy like that," Murphy answered.

"I saw him, too," I chimed up. "I thought he was in his thirties, but like Murphy said, it was hard to tell."

"Maybe our Romanescu has assumed the identity of the Hungarian guy," Murphy said. "He wouldn't be the first con-man to pretend to be someone else."

"Well, that would be one explanation," Hazeltine commented. "The rational one."

"What's your point, professor?"

"I'm not sure. I just find it interesting."

I knew what Hazeltine was getting at. Vampires aren't suppose to age. That's kind of the whole point of being a vampire.

"Well that pretty much exhausts what we know about Romanescu. Whether he's the same guy that came from Hungary in '56 or not, he's been awfully good at not leaving a paper trail."

"What about the churches?" Hazeltine asked. "Any luck with that."

"Professor Hazeltine made a suggestion that Romanescu might be using an abandoned church as a base," Murphy explained for the benefit of the group. He didn't mention that we suspected that that was where he had killed the girls and drained their blood.

"We've searched all of the buildings still standing that were formerly churches. Once we explained why, we didn't have much resistance from the owners. Unfortunately, nothing turned up."

"How did you come up with the list of buildings to search?" the professor asked.

"We used the tax rolls. We looked for anyplace that had been granted an exemption from taxes because they were a church. We also asked all the current congregations about their history. As I said, they were more than willing to cooperate when we explained why."

"What about synagogues?"

"Synagogues?" Murphy asked in puzzlement.

"Yes," Hazeltine said. "I don't think we can rule out places of worship just because they are non-Christian. It's the sacred nature that is important. Besides, there is a strong strain of Jewish Kabalah running through the occult. That might affect Romanescu's thinking. We know from some of the books he had in his possession that he was interested in aspects of the occult besides vampirism."

"I get your point, professor," Murphy said. "I'll see that it's looked into. Is it worth looking at religions other than Jewish?"

"It's hard to say. I'm not sure that there are any abandoned sacred buildings from other faiths. It couldn't hurt to look, though."

After that, things kind of broke up into a brainstorming session. Not that many good ideas came out of it. Murphy assigned some things to look into and a public education campaign was decided on, though that basically amounted to "don't go home with any strangers in dark clothing."

On the way out I cornered Hazeltine.

"What was that bit about Romanescu's age?" I asked when we were out of earshot of the rest of the group.

"Nothing. I just found it curious that neither you or Sergeant Murphy were capable of assigning Romanescu a definite age."

"Curious as in curious or curious as in you're not telling me everything. It sounds like you're starting to think Romanescu really is a vampire."

"Not at all. We both know there are no such things as vampires. I just found it interesting." And with that he left.

28.

The next day I got a call from Hazeltine. He sounded excited.

"What's up, Professor?"

"I've been talking to one of my colleagues in the history department who happens to be Jewish. He also acts as the unofficial historian of the local Jewish community. I thought that if anyone knew of an abandoned synagogue it would be him."

"I take it that he did?"

"You guessed it. He was only too willing to help when I told him why I was looking. Not only was he able to tell me of its existence, but he was able to get me the keys to the place."

"Do you want me to call Murphy?"

"Not just yet."

"Do you think that's wise?"

"It seems the current owners are a little sensitive about the place and would rather not involve the police if it can be avoided."

"Any idea why?"

"My colleague seemed to think that there are some negotiations going on with a developer and the owners don't want to jeopardize them with bad publicity. I thought we could check the place out ourselves and if we didn't find anything there'd be no reason to bring in the police. That was kind of a condition to get the keys."

I wasn't particularly happy with the situation, but Hazeltine was calling the shots. I certainly didn't think that we could afford not to check out the place. "OK. When do you want to check it out?"

"I can't get away until later this afternoon. How about if I meet you there around five?"

"That works for me." The professor agreed and gave me the address.

I was early and had to wait for the professor to show up, but I was able to find a parking place right in front of the address

Hazeltine had given me. That was just as well, as my leg was acting up. It hadn't given me much trouble all summer, but the last week or so it had stiffened up on me.

The block had obviously once been a fashionable one with solid looking brick and stone storefronts, but times had changed. There was a restaurant on the corner and an architectural firm down the block, but the rest of the buildings looked disused with the windows boarded up and the doors chained and padlocked. I could see, though, why a developer might be interested if he could buy up all the properties between the restaurant and the architect's office. The location wasn't bad and the surrounding neighborhood was slowly regaining some of its former vibrancy.

Even without the Star of David carved into the stonework above the door, it would have been easy to pick out which building was the synagogue. It was the only one without boarded up show windows. Instead, it had a short set of steps topped by a pair of imposing looking wooden doors. Above, on the stone lintel the date 1873 had been engraved. It had clearly once been a place of great pride for the local Jewish community.

My ruminations were interrupted by Hazeltine banging on the driver's side window.

"Good. You made it," he said as I stepped out of the car.

"I wouldn't miss it. You've got the keys?"

"Right here."

"OK. Let me get a couple of things out of the back." I unlocked the trunk and pulled out a heavy duty flashlight, the weighted kind that can double as a billy club in a pinch. "Did you bring a flashlight?"

"I've got a small one in my pocket. Not as big as yours."

I had an electric lantern in the trunk, so I pulled it out and gave it to the professor. I also stuffed a short pry bar in my jacket pocket just in case. I didn't mention to the professor the .38 automatic I was carrying in a should holster. I don't normally go around with a gun, but it seemed like a good idea to be prepared.

"So what's the story on this place?" I asked.

"The original synagogue was built on this site right before the Civil War. There were only a handful of Jewish families in town at the time. By the eighteen seventies there were about twenty families and they had enough money to support a rabbi. They also had the money to build a new synagogue, this building.

"By the late twenties the congregation had grown and was thinking about a new building again. One of the members who owned a prosperous furniture store offered a deal. He'd bought a nice piece of land for a new store, but after the Crash had decided not to expand. He said he'd swap the land for the old synagogue. They could start building right away, and he wouldn't take possession of the old building until the new synagogue was completed. It seemed like a good deal for everyone.

"Unfortunately, what with the Depression, building the new synagogue took longer than expected. By the time they were done, it was the eve of World War II, so nothing was ever done with the old building after they moved. By the time the war ended, the man who owned the furniture store had died. I gather the settlement of his estate was rather messy and things sat in the court for a few years. Meanwhile the building sat empty, or was just used for storage. The heirs have been trying to sell the building ever since, but, understandably, they've been particular about who they sell it to."

"It sounds like a perfect situation for Romanescu."

"Doesn't it, though. Shall we go inside?"

Hazeltine produced the key to the front door. Surprisingly, the lock turned freely as if it had been oiled recently. There was a light switch next to the door, but nothing happened when I flipped it. I turned on my flashlight. Hazeltine did the same with his lantern.

"Do you always carry your flashlight in you left hand?" the professor asked.

"Force of habit," I replied with a shrug. "Leaves the other hand free for a gun. Standard police training."

"I see." I think that was when it occurred to the professor that there might be the chance of personal danger in what we were doing.

I'd never been in a synagogue before, and I wasn't sure what to expect. Actually it didn't look that different from a church.

There was a lot of dark woodwork and plastered walls. Of course, all the more valuable or important fittings had been moved to the new synagogue when it opened. Still, there was a large, open room which had obviously been where the services were held. The seating was still in place, but pretty much everything else had been cleared out. There were no signs of Romanescu.

We walked down the narrow hall that ran towards the back of the building. There was another, smaller room, which from the shelves lining the walls had been a study or library. There was a room that might once have been an office off of the study.

We came to the back of the building where there was a set of stairs leading up. It looked like there might be another set of steps leading to the cellar.

"Up or down?" I asked.

"According to my colleague, upstairs there were quarters for the rabbi and a meeting room of sorts. My guess is that they wouldn't have been of interest to Romanescu for his rituals. I say we try the cellar first. We can always check the upstairs later."

"I was afraid you were going to say that."

As we had suspected, there was a door under the stairs that opened on another set of stairs leading to the cellar. This set was narrower, and more utilitarian in style. I shown the beam of my flashlight down the stairwell, but all we could see was a brick wall on the far side of the lower landing.

There wasn't any hand-railing, and my knee chose that moment to act up. I found myself going down the stairs one step at a time, always moving my right leg first. If Hazeltine noticed, he chose not to say anything.

The cellar was unfinished. Bare brick walls and exposed beams as far as we could see in the beams of our lights. Pillars that supported the upper stories broke up the space making it hard to see far. The floor had been paved in stone, but it looked like they had been laid directly on the earth below with no mortar or grout between stones.

What can I say. It was cold and damp as only an old cellar can be. Dust and cobwebs were everywhere. All in all, it was pretty creepy. I could tell the professor was feeling the same, because he was following me a little too closely for comfort.

"That direction should be right under the main room," Hazeltine said, pointing with his light. "That would be where he would conduct his rituals, if anywhere, as the most potent location."

It seemed the professor was right, because as we got closer I could make out the form of a large table, seven or eight feet long. It was hard to judge distances in the dark, but it looked like it was positioned directly under the center of the room above. The table was about three feet high, higher than a dinner table, more like a workbench.Someone had fitted leather straps to the top in just the right position to hold down the feet and hands of someone lying on the table. The table top was rough, but I thought I could make out a brownish stain about where a bound person's neck would be.

Looking away, I flashed my light along the side wall. There was another square table there, a crude affair of plywood and 2x4s. On top of it was a bunch of what looked like laboratory glassware along with some big ceramic vessels and copper basins. Strange symbols that I didn't recognize had been painted in various colors at the corners and the middle of the sides of the table.

"What's with this stuff, Professor?"

"It looks like our killer has been practicing alchemy. Not surprising, really. You never saw *Blood of the Vampyre's Daughter*, did you?"

"No. My taste runs more to John Wayne. Why?"

"The premise of the movie is that the blood of the descendents of Vlad Tepes contained an ingredient that was essential for a potion that would confer immortality. However, the blood had to be processed with a number of alchemical operations in order to work. There was a lot of nonsense about John Dee, Isaac Newton and other alchemists, but you get the idea."

"Isaac Newton, the apple guy?"

"Yes. He was obsessed with alchemy. Mathematics was only a sideline with him. In any case, it looks like our would be vampire has been taking the script of the movie literally."

"How did it end? The movie, I mean?"

"Badly, I'm afraid. Bodies everywhere," Hazeltine said reluctantly.

"I think we've seen enough to justify telling Murphy."

"Oh, I agree. But let's just poke around a little more."

I wasn't too keen on staying, but I couldn't abandon the professor. He started to move towards the front of the building. I stayed behind to examine the contents of the alchemical laboratory to see if I could find a clue to Romanescu's whereabouts. It was a pretty mixed lot, some modern, some almost medieval in appearance, bottles and jars of powders and liquids. There was a large flask containing a red liquid that I didn't want to think about.

Out of the corner of my eye I could see the beam from Hazeltine's lantern, but other than that and the circle of light cast by own flashlight the cellar was pitch dark. Suddenly he called out:

"Hey! Come over here. You've got to check this out."

29.

Hazeltine had been looking around behind the big coal furnace that had been used to heat the place. That was why we hadn't spotted it at first. I made my way through the cellar to where Hazaltine's lantern was pointing.

It was obvious that Romanescu hadn't just been using the synagogue for his rituals. He'd been living there, and quite recently. There was a pile of opened tin cans that had been tossed in a corner, and in a few of them there hadn't been time for the remnants to have dried out yet. There were other cans that hadn't been opened and a couple of plastic gallon water jugs. As I swung the beam of my flashlight around I spotted an old lawn chair and one of those little stoves campers use to heat up food. It was quite a contrast from the crude oriental splendor of his attic bedroom.

"He's been here, and not too long ago," I observed. "Looks like he still needs to eat and drink something other than blood." It was a pretty feeble joke.

"Yeah," the professor replied. "What do you make of that?"

His lantern flashed on a big wooden box that had been set up off the ground on a makeshift stand of bricks. It was a little over six feet long and maybe two feet wide and a foot and a half tall. It had been put together out of pine boards by someone who was no carpenter and it looked for all the world—well there's no other way to put it—like a coffin.

As I flashed my light on the interior I half expected to see Romanescu laying there. He wasn't, but it looked as if he had been. What there was, was a dirty blanket, and below that a thin layer of dirt.

"Is that what I think it is?" I asked.

"I'd say so," the professor replied. "It looks like Romanescu has been playing his role to the hilt."

"I don't know about that. It's still daylight out, isn't it? Shouldn't he be sleeping in the box here?"

"You're taking the whole vampire thing too literally. I'm afraid that that particular bit of lore was pretty much an invention of Bram Stoker. While it's true that direct sunlight is harmful to vampires, at least according to most of the legends, that doesn't mean they can't be active in the middle of the day, any more than we can't get be up in the middle of the night."

"Well it certainly looks like he's been sleeping here."

"The question is, where is he now?"

"I believe I can answer that," came a voice out of the darkness.

I spun around, catching a glimpse of a dark figure in the beam of the flashlight. It was Romanescu. I could have sworn that we had been alone in the cellar. Other than this nook behind the furnace, there weren't that many places to hide.

"I'm actually surprise that you've managed to find my little hiding place," Romanescu said, arrogance dripping from his voice as if we were a lesser order of creature.

"Oh, it wasn't that hard," Hazeltine responded. "You must remember, I've read the script to *Blood of the Vampyre's Daughter*. Hell, I wrote parts of it."

"Ah, Professor Hazeltine, I presume. So you've decided to throw in with your recent persecutors. You disappoint me. I would have thought better of you."

While his attention was focused on the professor I reached into my jacket for the automatic. I must not have been stealthy enough. It seemed that Romanescu crossed the space between us in an instant. I fired blindly, but at point blank range, before being bowled over. The pistol went flying off into the dark.

I'd dropped my flashlight, but it hadn't gone out, instead throwing it's beam so that I could see Romanescu standing over me, one of the paving stones held high over his head ready to crash down on me.

Hazeltine came to my rescue, launching a flying tackle at my assailant. The stone dropped, just missing my head, then Romanescu picked up the professor and hurled him across the cellar into one of the pillars.

Seemingly just as quickly as he had appeared, Romanescu was gone. I crawled over to where my flashlight lay, picking it up and swinging the beam wildly around trying to find Romanescu, but he was gone.

"Professor, are you OK?" I called out.

"I seem to have hit my head. There's blood. But other than that I think I'm alright. What about you?"

"I'll live. I think it's time to get out of here and call Murphy."

"I won't argue the point," the professor said. Surprisingly, he sounded almost chipper.

We must have looked a sight when we stumbled into the restaurant on the corner to use the phone. We were both covered with dirt and old coal dust. Hazeltine was bleeding from his forehead, but it thought looked worse than it actually was. I had to show my P.I. license and explain that I was calling the police before they would let me use the phone.

I got through to Murphy, and there was a squad car on the scene within a couple of minutes. The patrolman wasn't sure whether he should help us or hold us. Murphy made it a few minutes later and explained things.

While the patrolman used his first-aid kit to patch up Hazeltine's wound I told Murphy what had happened.

"You know it was a damned stupid thing going in there without backup, don't you? You let Romanescu get away." He didn't seem particularly concerned that we'd nearly gotten ourselves killed in the process.

"We weren't expecting trouble," I explained lamely. "The place looked like it was empty when we got there."

"So what did happen?"

"We were looking at the coffin thing. Suddenly, he just steps out of the dark. It was like he appeared from nowhere. I tried to get the drop on him, but he knocked me down."

"Just like that?"

"One minute he was standing ten feet away from me, the next he was on me. I didn't even see him move. I only had a chance to get off one shot before he knocked me down."

"You fired? Did you hit him?"

"I don't see how I could have missed. He was right in front of me, closer than you are now. But I must have. He didn't show any signs of being hit."

"What kind of gun?"

"A .38 automatic. Plenty of stopping power at that range."

"You probably missed. It was dark. You're lucky you didn't shoot yourself in the foot."

"I was holding the gun straight out in front of me, chest high almost. I'm not that bad of a shot."

"OK, OK. What happened then."

"He's standing over me holding this chunk of stone like he's planning to bash my head in and then the professor bulls into him."

"Hazeltine?"

"Yeah. Hazeltine. He probably saved my life. Anyway, Romanescu picks him up and tosses him about a dozen feet."

"And then?"

"And then he's gone. Just like he came. Neither one of us saw him go. He was just gone."

"Just gone. Like that?" I could hear the disbelief in Murphy's voice.

"Yeah."

"Well, we'll get him. At least now there can't be much doubt that Romanescu is our murderer. We've already got an A.P.B. out for him. What else did you find down there, besides this vampire and his coffin."

"I'm pretty sure that this is the place where the girls were killed. There's a whole alchemical laboratory down there and a table with straps to hold down his victims. I think I spotted a couple of bottles with what looks like blood. Maybe you can match it with one of the dead girls."

"Jeez Louize. Well, the lab boys are on the way. They'll give the place a going over."

Murphy wanted us to hang around. The lab team showed up and began hauling lights and a bunch of other equipment down to the cellar. A uniformed sergeant and a half dozen more patrolmen showed up and began searching the block. Hazeltine and I sat in my car waiting. I had a flask I kept in the glove box for emergencies. I pulled it out. I figured we both could use a bit of Dutch courage. The professor didn't disagree.

It seemed like hours, but was probably only thirty minutes when Murphy came over.

"I've got something I think you should see," was all he said.

We trundled back into the synagogue and down the backstairs to the cellar. It looked completely different now. The lab team had set up a bunch of portable lights, enough light to penetrate into every corner of the place. Now it was just a dirty old basement in an old building.

"I think this is how Romanescu got in and out." Murphy was pointing at a hole in the foundation wall about five feet high and three feet wide. Off to the side was a panel that had been covered in plaster and painted to make it look like part of the foundation. It was a pretty good attempt at camouflage.

"Where's it lead?"

"The building next door. They share a wall."

"Did you follow it?"

"What do you think?" Murphy sounded annoyed. "We followed it far enough to know that Romanescu is gone. There's another panel like this leading into the building on the other side of the one next door. There's probably a opening into the building beyond that."

"Romanescu did all of that?" Hazeltine asked.

"Naw. You find these a lot in old buildings in this part of town. Most of them date back to Prohibition if not earlier. A way for bootleggers to move things around without being seen."

"But into a synagogue?" I asked in disbelief.

"You never heard of Meyer Lansky or Bugsy Siegel?" Murphy asked. "Romanescu must have found them when he was looking for a place for his rituals. It was an ideal setup for him. Most of the buildings on this block are empty. He could bring in the girls and take out the bodies without anyone finding this place."

"Yeah. Real slick."

"It's going to take the lab boys weeks to check out all those chemicals and stuff, but you were right about one thing. They confirmed that the stain on the table is blood. They're pretty sure it's human blood, too. They also found the thing he used to make the wounds. It's a little piece of steel with two prongs and a fitting that could hook up to a rubber hose. It looks like this is the place where Anna Smerchek and the others were killed."

"I'm not sure whether to be happy or sad," the professor said.

"Look at it this way, Professor. Without your help we might not have found this place. Romanescu won't be performing any more of his rituals and it's only a matter of time before we find him."

"That's something, at least."

"One other thing. The lab boys found a spent bullet. Probably a .38. Yours most likely. It ended up in one of the pillars. Right over here." Murphy went over and pointed out the hole where they'd found it. "It's about four feet off the ground, right about the level you fired from. Where were you standing?"

"About here," I said, stepping over to a spot about ten feet from the pillar.

"Hard to see how you could have missed at that range, but the lab boys say there's no chance that the shot hit anyone before it hit the pillar. Must have been pure luck on Romanescu's part."

"Did you find my automatic?"

"You don't still have it?" Murphy asked.

"No. It went flying when Romanescu ran into me."

"Well, it's not here now. I'll tell the lab boys to keep a lookout for it."

I wasn't too happy about losing the gun. It was the only one I had, but that wasn't what was bothering me. What was bothering me was that Romanescu might have picked it up.

We poked around a bit more looking for my pistol, but we were only getting in the way of the lab techs. Finally Murphy said he needed a beer. Neither the professor or I disagreed.

30.

One thing I like about this town is that, at least in the older parts of it, you never have to go far to find a tavern. The restaurant on the corner had put out the closed sign and turned off the lights, but Murphy said he knew of a place a couple of blocks over. It wasn't far, so we decided to walk.

I can't remember the name of the joint, the sign out front just said "BAR," but it was one of those neighborhood taverns that have existed pretty much unchanged since the end of Prohibition. This one was typical, a small brick building on a corner in a neighborhood of frame houses. It was the kind of place where most of the clientele are regulars, they serve decent burgers from eleven till eight, they drink a lot of Seven and Sevens and brandy Old Fashioneds, and on Saturday morning you can get a good Bloody Mary. You can get a Bloody Mary on Sunday morning, too, for that matter. The juke box doesn't have anything newer than ten years old on it, mostly stuff like Patsy Cline and Frank Sinatra.

When we stepped inside, the place didn't disappoint. There was a long bar running along one wall and a couple of tables along the other. The only patrons in the place were two older geezers nursing beers at the far end of the bar away from the door to be out of the draft on the off chance someone should come in. They were having a discussion about the university's football team, which from what I could overhear was mostly comparing players who hadn't played in a decade. The bartender was interjecting comments occasionally, but seemed more concerned with polishing the glassware. They all looked up when we came in, but then went back to what they had been doing. There was a TV mounted up in the corner, but in that kind of place they only turn it on for football, basketball, or baseball. No one was playing that night.

The bar curved around in the front of the building, so we parked ourselves around the angle so we could see each other better. The bartender came over and Murphy ordered three taps and dropped a fin on the bar. The bartender brought the beers over and then went back to ignoring the geezers.

Murphy didn't say much as he sipped his beer. Neither did I. The professor just kept quiet, a thoughtful look on his face. Finally Murphy spoke up.

"Seems like you've got something on your mind, Professor. Want to let us in on it?"

Hazeltine took a sip of his beer then replied. "It's just that I've been thinking."

"That much is obvious," Murphy said.

"We've been operating under the assumption that Romanescu is just this guy whose under the delusion that he's a vampire, or that he is becoming a vampire or whatever. Right?"

"That's what you've been telling us all along, isn't it?" Murphy asked. He sounded a little annoyed, but I mostly chalked that up to stress.

"Yeah. And that's what I thought, too. It makes sense after all. He's been going around acting like a Bela Lugosi wannabe. He certainly has all the hallmarks of a psychopathic killer."

"OK. So what's your point?"

"OK, this is the part you're not going to like. We all know there are no such things as vampires, right. But what if—just what if—we're wrong? What if Romanescu really is, or is becoming, a real vampire?"

"Professor, I'm starting to think you're the one that's nuts. How badly did you hit your head when he tossed you around?"

"Just hear me out for a minute. I'm not talking about the vampire of fiction. I'm not saying that he can turn himself into a bat or a puff of smoke or anything of the other stuff out of the movies. But what if there really was something to all the old legends and there was a way for a man to become immortal or at least retard aging? What if the process also gave that person unnatural strength and speed, and maybe the ability to control people's perceptions, at least to a limited degree? And what if the key ingredient for this process was human blood? Wouldn't that fit our definition of a 'vampire'?"

"There ain't no such thing as vampires, Professor, and there ain't no real magic, either," Murphy protested. "What you're talking about is just plain crazy."

"Maybe you're right, Sergeant. That certainly is the rational way to look at things. But what if I'm right? Even a little bit? I've poked around a lot of old archives and writing and let me tell you there are some pretty odd bits and pieces lying around, things that can't be explained in nice rational ways. Is it all really just a bunch of nonsense?"

"You don't really believe this, do you, professor?" I asked. The discussion between Murphy and Hazeltine had been getting a little heated, and I wanted to cool it down. I motioned to the bartender to bring another round.

"Maybe not. Like I said, I just got to thinking. But let's look at the facts about Romanescu."

"Like what?" I asked.

"Like the fact that you shot him at point blank range and it didn't affect him? Let's start there."

"It was dark. He was rushing me." I countered.

"At the time, did you think you hit him?"

"Yeah."

"OK. Maybe you did miss. Or maybe—the bullet just went through him without hurting him. But let's go on to my next point. After you shot him I tried to help you and he just tossed me like I was nothing—like he had superhuman strength."

"You went after Romanescu? I still find that hard to believe," Murphy said in surprise.

"Yeah. He was a real terror. Might have saved my life," I said coming to the professor's defense.

"Until he tossed me like a basketball," Hazeltine demurred.

"I didn't know you had it in you, Professor," Murphy said.

"Well it's been awhile since I did any hand to hand combat. Not since Korea," the professor's voice suddenly as chilly as Chosen. "But the point still is he tossed me a dozen feet or more."

I had to give this point to Hazeltine. Romanescu had knocked me down and thrown the professor halfway across the cellar.

Even granting that Hazeltine only weighed a hundred fifty at most, it had taken a lot of strength.

"You read about people doing amazing feats of strength under stress," Murphy argued. "It's the adrenaline."

"Maybe. But what about the way he suddenly appeared and just as suddenly disappeared?"

"You saw the tunnel."

"Even if he did use the tunnel, he wasn't moving like a normal human," Hazeltine said.

"It did seem like he wasn't there one moment and was there the next," I chimed in again. "He went away just the same way."

"It was dark. Between your two flashlights you could barely see down there. He could have been hiding in the dark behind one of the pillars all the time," Murphy responded.

"Alright. You weren't there, so you don't know what we saw."

"Look, I understand what you're saying, but maybe it was the just way you saw it. It was a high stress situation, it was dark, things happened fast. It could be you imagined things happened differently than the way they really happened."

"Again, maybe you're right. But what about the age thing. Romanescu, even if he is in terrific shape, wasn't acting like any fifty year old that I know of, and trust me, I know what a fifty year old moves like."

"We don't know his age. We don't even know if this guy is the same Vladimir Romanescu that the State Department let in back in '56. He could be somebody completely different. That might not even be his real name. The guy could be a complete phony. Maybe he was born Fred Smith in Hoboken in 1949 and just assumed the identity of Vladimir Romanescu. Hell, he might even have just picked that name out of a hat."

"I can't argue with that," the professor continued. "You might be right on each and every point. That would certainly be the rational way of looking at things. But what if I'm right, even just a little?"

About this time I glanced at the two geezers at the far end of the bar. They must have overheard our conversation because they were looking our way and whispering to the bartender.

"OK. What if you are right? Even a little?" Murphy asked. "This guy, whoever or whatever he is, is still using young girls as his personal blood bank, and we've got to stop him. We can't just walk away because this guy is a vampire or some other kind of monster."

"No, we can't," the professor agreed. "But what I'm saying we should be thinking about is that if Romanescu really is becoming a vampire or some other sort of supernatural being, that ordinary measures may not be enough to stop him and we should be prepared for that eventuality."

"OK. So how do you kill a vampire? I can't very well order a case of silver bullets, can I?"

"They wouldn't work, anyway. Silver bullets are for lycanthropes."

"Lycan-whats?" Murphy asked.

"Werewolves. Silver bullets are for werewolves. At least in popular legend as depicted in the movies."

"OK. What works for vampires?"

"According to the movies sunlight, holy water, crosses, a wooden stake to the heart. But that's just Hollywood."

"What about the legends, the real ones?" I asked.

"Cutting off the head, particularly if you bury it with the body with the head facing backwards. Or a wodden stake to the heart. That one Bram Stoker and Hollywood got right."

"I don't think the department will let me issue battle axes to patrolmen. Besides, the people in this town are spooked enough without seeing a bunch of cops carrying axes."

"OK. Maybe not regular police officers. But it might not be a bad idea to keep a machete or something in the trunk of your car and a mallet and some tent stakes. Heck, even the holy water and cross thing might be worth giving a shot. It's clear that Romanescu, whatever he is, has gotten at least some of his ideas from popular literature and movies, including my own book, I'm sad to say. Things like that might slow him down enough that more mundane means to work."

"You're serious about chopping off his head?"

"Well, the good thing about that is it works whether he's a vampire or not."

"Yeah. I'll keep that in mind when the time comes."

"Look. Maybe I'm all wet. It could just be that I'm all psyched up after our run in with Romanescu. He was probably just some worked up crazy guy taking on a gimp and an out of shape academic. But if he's not, I think we'd be wise to be prepared." Hazeltine seemed dead serious about his suggestion.

"Yeah, you might be right, Professor. But we've still got to find him, and I'm willing to try a few rounds from my service revolver before I pull out the holy water and crucifix."

There didn't seem to be an answer to that. We sat nursing our beers in silence. Finally Murphy said, "It's getting late, Professor, and I have a feeling I'll be busy in the morning."

31.

I woke up the next morning to a ringing phone. It was Murphy. He didn't sound happy.

"He struck again last night."

"Romanescu?" I asked groggily.

Murphy didn't even bother to comment on the obviousness of my question.

"Yeah. Marie Bertoli, walking home from her job as a waitress. Her body was found less than two blocks from her parent's home."

"Bertoli? Any relation—?"

"Yeah. His niece."

Luigi Bertoli had been on the force until his retirement. He'd been an old school cop, hard-nosed on the job, but kind and gentle off-duty. He raised tomatoes and had played Santa for the kids at the department Christmas party until he retired a couple of years earlier.

"What happened?"

"It's hard to say. Looks like he may just have grabbed her off the street and dragged her into an alley. It must have happened while we were drinking beer. We've got to get this guy."

There was a pause as if Murphy was expecting me to say something, but I didn't bother to reply.

"Look, just get down here. The D.A.'s called a meeting. And see if you can get Hazeltine to come, too. He seems to be the only one who' got a clue as to what Romanescu is up to."

"This is what we know," Murphy said. Behind him there was a bulletin board with photos of the crime scene. They were pretty gruesome. There were more cops in the room than at the last meeting. The chief and the D.A. were there, as well. "Marie Bertoli, aged twenty, was walking home from her job as a waitress. According to the manager, she left the restaurant around 10:30. Her parent's home where she lived is only a half-mile or so from the restaurant and she usually walked unless the weather was really bad. When that happened, the manager usually gave her a ride, but that meant waiting around at the restaurant."

"She couldn't wait?" one of the older detectives asked. It sounded personal, but then he'd probably worked with Luigi Bertoli for years. "We got a mad man running around and she couldn't wait a half-hour?"

"Her father said she had a class first thing this morning and she wanted to get home and go to bed," Murphy explained.

"What was she studying?" someone asked, an irrelevant question now.

"She was taking classes at the technical school. She was studying to be a nurse. Getting back to the case, when she hadn't come home by eleven, her mother called the restaurant. They said she'd already left. Her father went looking for her. He was the one who found her. As far as we can tell, she was pulled into an alleyway between two buildings and her throat was cut, a neat little wound right across the jugular vein. There was a lot of blood."

"Excuse me, but why do you think this was Romanescu?" the professor asked quietly.

"The restaurant where she worked is only a half-dozen blocks from the synagogue. A young woman, that much blood, who else would it be but Romanescu? Besides, we have a witness who says he saw a man in black shortly after the crime. The description matches Romanescu."

"It was dark last night. I don't doubt that the witness saw a man in dark clothing, but can we be sure it was Romanescu?"

"We got lucky. There was a footprint at the scene. The same lab tech that was at the synagogue was at the scene where Marie was found. He remembered that he had taken a photo of a footprint in the dirt of the basement floor. He compared that photo with the one he took at the crime scene. They match. According to the tech, it's a pretty unusual footprint, too, very long but quite narrow, size 11B. Satisfied?"

"Yes. I just wanted to make sure," Hazeltine said. It sounded as if he had more on his mind.

"Good," Murphy said, then, "Why is it so important, Professor?"

"Because this victim doesn't match the others," Hazeltine answered. "She's living at home with her parents, she's going to school, she's working—I take it she wasn't into the occult or anything like that?"

"She was a good girl, Professor. You said it yourself, home, school, work. She didn't have time for any nonsense. Besides, she was a good Catholic."

"That's just my point. Look at the other three victims. One was a runaway, one was living away from home for the first time in her life, and the other, well it looks like she had bought into the same delusion that Romanescu has. But this one was, as you said, a good girl."

"Anna Smerchek wasn't a runaway or delusional," I protested.

"No, but she was obviously fascinated with the occult. We have every reason to believe that she went back to the House of Esoteric Wisdom after the time with her boy friend. That's what's different about this case. The others came to Romanescu. He didn't have to search them out. He didn't have to snatch them off the street. Besides, the manner of her death is different. Gone is the careful staging of the body. Gone is the blood carefully drained from the body. There are no elements of magic surrounding the killing. It's all changed."

"What are you getting at, Professor?" Murphy asked impatiently.

"Before, with the first three killings, and with the one in Columbus if that was Romanescu, he wanted the blood because it was part of some ritual, some alchemical process, some mad scheme of transformation. If we accept the fact that he's playing out a fantasy based on *Blood of the Vampyre's Daughter*, then the first three murders were done to obtain the blood necessary for his transformation into a vampire. With this last killing that's not the case. The question is, Why?"

"How should I know? I'm not nuts. What does it matter, anyway?" Murphy said, practically shouting.

"It matters because we want to stop this guy, that's why," the professor shouted back. "Before, Romanescu was working within limitations. Each killing had to be carefully planned and executed according to the strictures of the ritual. That's no longer the case. Why isn't that the case? Because Romanescu, at least in his own mind, has already become a vampire. He didn't kill that girl last night because it was part of a ritual. He killed her because he was feeding!"

"That's crazy, Professor."

"That is exactly the point I've been trying to make. It doesn't matter what Romanescu is. What matters is what he thinks he is. And judging from this last killing I'd say he thinks that he's now a real full-fledged, blood-sucking vampire. That makes him even more dangerous than what he was before."

"How do you figure that?"

"Before, he had to be careful. Before, he had to operate within the rules of the ritual. He had to lure his victims into his lair, because what he had to do couldn't be done hurriedly or in the open. Now, he's not operating under those same constraints. That means he can just grab someone off the streets, sever their neck vein, feed on a little blood and be off. At this point, I'm not even convinced that his victims will have to be young women. Anybody might do for a midnight snack."

"Great. Just what we need. Any other good news, Professor?"

"Maybe, maybe not. We've been looking for Romanescu under the assumption that he needed some sort of sacred or consecrated location to perform his rituals. At the time it was a valid assumption. That's why we found him at the abandoned synagogue. Now that he believes he is transformed, that may not be the case. He could be holed up anywhere."

"I really didn't mean it, Professor," Murphy said. "About the good news."

"It may not be as bad as that. Remember the makeshift coffin with dirt that we found in the synagogue's cellar. That's a sign that Romanescu buys into the notion that he must rest in some of his native soil during the day. That's something straight out of Bram Stoker, by the way. He's probably made provisions for this by hiding coffins around the city. How many places can you hide a box that size?"

"I get what you're saying."

"And if we can find some of them, we can restrict his movements even more. He doesn't have a car. He can only move at night. He has to get back to one of his coffins by daylight—"

"It's a plan, Professor. It's a plan," Murphy said. He almost sounded cheerful.

"I'd like to say something, if I may," the D.A. interrupted. "First, I'd like to thank you all for your good work. I'm sure it's appreciated. But it sounds to me as if you actually are starting to believe that this—Romanescu—really is a vampire. That's absurd."

"I'm sorry if that's what it sounds like," Hazeltine apologized. "As I said, it's not what he is that matters. It's what he thinks he is. And that's the only way we're going to catch him. We have to get inside his mind."

"I understand that, Professor Hazeltine. What I want to make clear, though, is that what you have been discussing stays within this room. We can't have word of this discussion leaking out to the public. Things are bad enough as it is with four young women dead. The city is on the verge of a full blown panic. If the idea gets out there that the police are treating Romanescu as if he were an actual vampire—well you can imagine what will happen."

"I think we all understand the gravity of the situation, sir," Murphy responded. "You can trust the discretion of everyone in this room."

"As long as we all understand that," the D.A. said. "I'll leave you to the details. I have a press conference to prepare for."

The D.A. held his press conference. They played portions of it on the 6 and 10 o'clock news. He told the reporters that there was a dangerous and clever maniac on the loose and that people should take precautions, especially at night, but that the police department was devoting its full resources to catching this criminal. He made no mention of vampires, coffins, or blood.

Not that it did him much good. It seems the two geezers from the bar had heard more than we thought. Either that, or someone from the department, or the D.A.'s office, or the Medical Examiner's office, or someone else involved had leaked the story that the police were treating Romanescu as a vampire and were looking for coffins that might be scattered around town.

The good that came out of it was that people looking in cellars and abandoned buildings actually managed to turn up two of the coffins. Hazeltine had looked particularly self-satisfied when Murphy told him about the discoveries.

The down side of the search was that three more bodies came to light. They were all young girls, all had been listed as missing or runaways. It didn't help much when the M.E. decided that they had all probably been killed months before Anna Smerchek had disappeared.

32.

In October things just got worse. Romanescu claimed two more victims, one in the first week, the second, ten days later. As Hazeltine had predicted, Romanescu was now acting as an opportunistic feeder, not taking his prey in carefully planned attacks, but instead killing at random. The professor had been right about another thing, too. He no longer was restricting himself to young, isolated women. The first October victim had been a fifty year old woman who worked as a bartender at a downtown hotel. She'd been taken on the way to her car after work. The second victim was a man in his mid-thirties, an accountant who'd been on his way home from a late night at the office.

The woman had been taken by surprise. The M.E.'s report said there were no signs of a struggle. Romanescu had come up behind her and slit her throat before she'd known what was happening. She'd died almost instantly.

The second attack had gone differently. The accountant had served in Vietnam and hadn't gone down without a fight. He'd been a strong man, too, fit and in his prime, despite his occupation. There'd been quite a struggle, loud enough for someone to call the cops, not that that did the accountant any good. Romanescu had melted away in the night before the patrolmen arrived.

According to the crime lab crew, not all the blood they found at the crime scene had been the victim's. At least Romanescu could still bleed. Small consolation to the accountant's wife and two kids.

There'd been a number of near misses, too, incidents where the targets had managed to escape, mostly by luck. The interviews afterwards all had the same story line. Romanescu had appeared, seemingly out of thin air, somehow the intended victim managed to get away and when they looked back, their attacker was gone, vanished as mysteriously as he had appeared. One nearly hysterical witness claimed that she had seen

Romanescu climb up the side of a building. A return to the scene had revealed a fire-escape ladder leading to the roof.

One of the men who had been attacked had been carrying a concealed pistol. He hadn't had a permit for it, but the police weren't pressing the point. They had bigger issues to deal with. The guy said that he got off five shots at less than six feet. He claimed he couldn't have missed, but they hadn't had any effect on his attacker. They dug five slugs out of a wall that matched the caliber of his gun. They'd been bunched in a fairly tight grouping, about what you'd expect if someone was shooting at a man-sized target a half-dozen feet away. Yet he seemed to have missed Romanescu. Either that, or they'd gone right through him without doing any damage. When I read the report I thought back to my own encounter in the cellar of the synagogue. I hadn't thought I'd missed, either.

People were going crazy, calling for something to be done, calling for a curfew, calling for the National Guard to be brought in, calling for anything that might end the terror. The D.A. had been worried about a panic. Well, now he had it with a vengeance.

The press, as was to be expected, were calling for heads to roll, anybody's head. Not that the press were helping matters any. One paper was running headlines asking whether there was a conspiracy of silence on the part of the police; that they knew more about Romanescu than they had let on; and implying that what they were concealing was that the city really was dealing with a vampire. Of course all the rationales the paper gave, that Romanescu had a radiation induced mutation, that he was the result of some a soviet experiment to create a super soldier, or that he was the product of some secret government project, sounded like plot lines from some 1950s B-movies. Hazeltine, our expert on such matters, even thought he knew which movies had served as the basis for each theory.

None of this, however, was helping to stop Romanescu. Murphy wasn't looking good. He was working seven days a week, working the day shift and then spending half the night driving around on patrol. The professor and I weren't doing much better because we were joining him half the time.

That's how we happened to be riding with him the night the two cops were killed. Officially, neither one of us had any sort of real standing, but things had gotten to the point where the chief wasn't about to turn down any offered help.

I was sitting in the front passenger seat paying attention to the radio while Murphy drove us around in circles in the student section. We were in an unmarked car that wouldn't have fooled anyone. Hazeltine was in the back seat looking nervous. I'm not sure why he was there. It wasn't really his business. For Murphy, it was his job, and as for myself, well I'd been hired to find Anna Smerchek so that made it my business, but no one would have thought the less of the professor if he'd stayed out of it. Yet there he was, leaning forward in the back seat, white knuckles showing as he grasped the seatback in front of him. I didn't have much in common with the professor, and I probably never will, but I was really coming to like and respect the guy.

The radio squawked out a request for backup from a patrol car. The address was about seven blocks down and five streets over. The patrolman said that he'd seen something in an alley way. There wasn't any question as to what that "something" was. Dispatch ordered another car to respond and come in from the other end of the alley and then called for additional backup. Neither officer was to get out of their car until it arrived. Murphy called dispatch to tell them we were responding and then sped towards the address.

Unfortunately, the patrolmen hadn't followed orders. It couldn't have taken us more than five minutes to get there. When we arrived at the end of the alley we could see one of the squad cars blocking it, it's red lights flashing and the driver's door hanging open. At the far end of the alley there were more flashing lights from the other car.

Murphy grabbed the riot gun from where it was clipped between the seats almost before we had stopped. I hadn't recovered my gun, but Murphy had lent me his spare, a .25 automatic. Not much stopping power, but at that point I was starting to doubt if anything would drop Romanescu. I turned in the seat to tell the professor to stay in the car, but he had already hopped out. He was carrying an old machete, an ugly looking thing. I found myself wondering if maybe he had the right idea. I swung out, planted my foot, and almost went down as my knee gave out. Cursing, I limped after Murphy and the professor.

We found the first officer about thirty feet down the alley, thrown up against the door of a garage. His neck had been broken. It looked like he'd been tossed like a rag doll. I checked his pulse to make sure, but just shook my head when Murphy glanced my way.

Murphy started walking down the middle of the alley, the riot gun held up to his shoulder, his flashlight pointing along the barrel. I had a flashlight, too, which I was shining crazily this way and that trying to illuminate all the shadows. The professor followed, walking backwards and holding the machete up so it would be ready.

We could see something lying on the ground silhouetted in the headlights of the squad at the far end. It was pitch black except for our flashlights, the headlights of the squads at each end and the strobe of their red lights on top. It was an old residential block, and the alley was flanked by high fences broken by the occasional garage door. Wherever the flashlight beams weren't was in dark shadows.

The alley was only about a hundred yards long, but it seemed like it took us forever to reach the far end. By the time we got there my leg was killing me. The "something" we had seen was the body of the other officer. His throat had been slashed, nearly severing his neck. I didn't even bother to check for a pulse.

We stood still for a moment, listening to the dark. Somewhere, it could have been the next block, it could have been just the other side of the fence there was a sound like a trash can being tipped over. Murphy swung the riot gun in that direction, but then there was nothing.

It seemed like an eternity, but it was probably only thirty seconds, before a couple more squads pulled up. There were a couple of minutes of confusion as everybody got sorted out. I don't blame the patrolmen, who could with two uniformed bodies on the ground and three wild eyed characters, one holding a shot gun and another with a machete standing back to back in the middle as if they were ready to take on the world. A uniformed sergeant showed up, recognized Murphy and took charge, sending the newcomers to cruise the neighborhood. It didn't do much good, Romanescu was gone.

The meat wagon and the crime lab crew showed up as did the watch lieutenant. There wasn't much for us to do anymore. Not that we'd really done anything earlier.

From what the lab guys were able to put together, the first officer must had gotten out of his car and seen something in the alley. He got off three rounds before being tossed against the garage. The second officer must have arrived on the scene just as this was ending and gotten out to respond. Somehow, Romanescu had run the hundred yard length of the alley and slashed the patrolman's throat before he even had a chance to get his gun out. Should they have stayed in their cars until backup arrived? Sure, in hindsight, but I'd have probably acted the same. I'm sure Murphy would have.

So that was October. Four dead, including two cops. Not a good month. And then came Halloween.

33.

For Halloween, the city was on a virtual lockdown. There'd been a lengthy debate on whether the mayor and the city council had the authority to ban trick-or-treating, but it hadn't really mattered, no one was letting their kids out after dark and even if they had, those kids would have found no doors opening for them. A curfew had been proposed, but it had been deemed unworkable. Still, it had been strongly suggested in the media that no one travel the streets alone that night. Most people seemed to be heeding the warning.

Private Halloween parties still went on, but fewer than normal. Several churches offered all-night slumber parties where no one would be allowed to leave until the dawn. Bars that normally made a big deal of the night had scaled back their plans, though one enterprising hotel was offering a package deal on a night's accommodation plus a costume party complete with a live band for those who absolutely felt the need to dress up and act silly. One of the local papers reported that there had been a run on Dracula costumes at the costume rental shop.

There was a feeling throughout the city that Halloween was going to provide a climax to of some sort, though there was no real reason to think this. Romanescu hadn't delivered any manifesto proclaiming the apocalypse. In fact, unlike most fanatics, he hadn't bothered to contact any of the media either to claim or deny responsibility for the deaths.

The police department was taking Halloween seriously. All officers had been ordered to report for duty. I didn't heard of any complaints about pulling double shifts. After the fiasco in the alley, every patrol car carried at least two officers, in the campus area that was bumped to three. Some recently retired cops offered their services for the night which augmented even that number. The police armory had been emptied and each squad was equipped with at least two riot guns. Someone had even checked out the vintage Thompson that was a relic from Prohibition. There was a lively debate as to which type of round would be most effective in the riot guns, birdshot, buckshot, or slugs. Most cars were hedging their bets and carrying all three.

Hazeltine and I were riding along with Murphy, Murphy doing the driving while I sat in the passenger seat cradling the shotgun and working the radio. Hazeltine was in the back. He'd refused a gun, though Murphy had offered him one. Instead he had brought along a black Gladstone bag like doctors used to carry. When asked, he'd said that it held sandwiches and a thermos of coffee. I expected there were other things in it as well, like holy water and wooden stakes. At that point, no one would have questioned either.

The early part of the night was quiet enough. Occasionally the radio would crackle with the report of a sighting, but those turned out to be kids trying to be daring. Even that died down after ten. Kids might be crazy, but they're not stupid.

That left us cruising back and forth in the night. Unlike the marked squad cars, we didn't have a fixed territory to patrol. Instead, after talking it over, we had decided to drive around an area roughly bounded by the House of Esoteric Wisdom, the abandoned synagogue, and the edge of the campus, that being where Romanescu had been seen most often.

It was pretty eerie. The streets were mostly abandoned. There weren't any pedestrians out and very few cars on the streets. Most people had turned off their porch lights to discourage trick-or-treaters and so as not to attract attention to themselves. Add to that the fact that it was a damp cold night with a fog starting to descend and it felt like the night was closing in around us leaving us in an isolated bubble lit only by the dashboard lights.

"Either of you guys want a sandwich?" Hazeltine asked. His voice had been soft, but it still startled us. "I've got ham and swiss on rye and pastrami."

"I'll take ham," Murphy answered.

I said, "Pastrami sounds good. Is the coffee hot?"

"It should be," the professor responded. He rummaged around his black bag and handed a couple of sandwiches wrapped in wax paper forward to the front seat. Murphy pulled over to the curb, leaving the motor running and the lights on while we ate. The professor had brought a couple of cups for the coffee and passed the thermos around.

"Do you think Romanescu will show tonight?" Murphy asked between bites.

"Hard to say," the professor answered nervously. "There's nothing in particular tying Halloween to the vampire legend. It's more of a Celtic thing. Still, in the popular imagination, the two have come to be linked along with witches and goblins and all the other things that go bump in the night."

"So you still think that this Romanescu guy is just acting out all the things he's seen in the movies?"

"Do you really want to think otherwise, Sergeant?" Hazeltine countered. "What does that leave us with? Do you really want to go there?"

Murphy just grunted. We all knew what the professor meant. Somehow it was more comforting to believe that Romanescu was just a crazed maniac with a delusion fed by cheap movies than to accept the fact that—well that he was a real vampire. That kind of put a end to the conversation and we finished our sandwiches in silence.

Despite the fact that it was a damp and chilly night, we'd rolled the windows down part way so that we would be able to hear anything that was going on. I glanced at the clock in the dashboard. It was just a few minutes before midnight. My knee was starting to ache from sitting in one position too long. The fog seemed to be muffling any sound. Somewhere, in one of the houses a stereo was playing a little too loud, but even that was barely audible.

Suddenly, there was a cry, like a stifled scream.

"Did you hear that?" I asked.

Murphy held up his hand and whispered, "Quiet."

For the next minute we listened to the stillness. The cry wasn't repeated.

"I think it came from over there," Murphy said. "I think we should check it out. Call it in." He didn't wait for a reply, but was out of the car. The professor followed after him, clutching the black bag in his right hand. I got on the radio, gave our location and said we were investigating.

By this time, Murphy was maybe forty feet ahead of me. My knee was acting up and I was trying to catch up with a stiff leg, the riot gun held up before me.

Murphy had stopped to listen at an alleyway separating two older apartment buildings. Neither the professor or I said anything. Murphy turned on his big flashlight and swung the beam up the alley. There was the usual clutter of garbage cans and boxes casting shadows, but some thirty feet or so down the alley there was a dark mound sprawled on the ground.

A window on the second floor of one of the apartment buildings opened and a figure leaned out to see what was going on. Murphy cried out, "Get back inside and lock your doors and windows." The window slammed shut with a crash.

We edged forward towards the mound, Murphy waving his flashlight from side to side and me limping along trying to cover the darkness with the shotgun.

Hazeltine had a flashlight of his own which he used on the mound, revealing it to be a young woman in her mid-twenties. A dark pool was forming underneath her neck. The professor reached down to check for a pulse. He shook his head. He dipped his finger in the pool of blood, felt it between his fingers.

"It's still warm," he said calmly. "With the ground as cold as it is, it can't have been long since she was killed. Romanescu may still be around."

Murphy shown his flashlight up the alley, but there didn't seem to be anything there. I had the shotgun up to my shoulder following the beam and wondered if it would be enough to stop him. I couldn't remember what kind of shells I'd loaded it with.

All we could see in the light from the flash were the usual detritus you find in alleys, garbage cans, boxes, an abandoned sofa, all casting weird shadows against the grimy bricks of the flanking apartments. The three of us edged forward, step, step, limp. The beam caught on a patch of blackness darker than the rest. The blackness shifted, then stood up. It was Romanescu, his pale face lit up by the flashlight. He took off running down the alley.

I fired the shotgun, but I was probably too far for it to be effective even if I had had time to aim. Murphy just took off after him, his service revolver in one hand and the flashlight in the other. Hazeltine was only a step behind him, black bag in hand. I worked the slide of the shotgun to put another shell in and limped stiff-legged after.

34.

We reached the other end of the alley, which opened out onto one of the major arterials that ran past the campus, and spilled out onto the sidewalk looking in all directions for Romanescu. The fog had closed in, but after a moment Hazeltine called out, "That's him!" and started running towards the left. Murphy followed after, and I limped along clutching the shotgun and wincing with every step. It occurred to me that we should have called in backup as soon as we had spotted Romanescu, but it was too late for that now. Hopefully, the shot I had fired from the riot gun would bring support.

Romanescu had had about a fifty yard head start, but he was fitter than any of us and we were in danger of losing him. He reached the corner of the block and took another left. When Murphy and the professor reached the corner he was out of our sight. They stood in the intersection staring into the fog and listening for a sound that did not come until I caught up with them.

"What now?" I asked breathlessly. The street was mostly commercial with businesses catering to the students on the campus. Even without the fog there were plenty of alleyways for Romanescu to hide in.

The professor tapped my arm and pointed at the building on the corner. At one time it had been a church, later a funeral parlor. Sometime in the sixties it had changed hands and became a pool hall/dance club known as The Church Pew that featured bands on weekend nights. That business had ended when the owner had lost his liquor license for serving underage students one too many times. For the last few months it had been closed. I could see what Hazeltine was thinking; it was just the sort of place that would appeal to Romanescu.

"You think he's in there?"

"Look at the door," he said, pointing at a metal door on the side of the building that must have served as an emergency exit. There was no handle on the outside, and there had been a hasp and padlock securing it, but the hasp had been torn loose from the bolts holding it to the door frame and was hanging free.

Murphy gave a tug on the hasp and the door swung open a few inches.

"You'd better stay out here, Professor," Murphy said. "Try to flag down any squad that comes by."

"You think I'm staying out here by myself," Hazeltine protested. "I might be wrong about Romanescu being inside. Where would that leave me?"

"Suit yourself," Murphy replied. "Ready?"

He didn't wait for an answer, but pulled the door all the way open. He entered, flashlight in his left hand and pistol in the other. I followed behind, just like in the movies, holding the shotgun at the ready and pointing it this way and that in the darkness. The professor came last. He had ditched his black bag and held a big silver cross in his right hand and clutched a glass vial in his left.

We were in a big room that had previously been the chapel. A few security lights provided enough illumination that we could see our surroundings. There was a small stage at one end where the altar had originally been. Tables and church pews line the dance floor in front of the stage. The choir loft at the end opposite the stage had been extended along both sides of the room to form a balcony ringing the dance floor. A bar ran along most of the wall underneath the loft. Someone had left a "Hamm's" sign still plugged in providing a blue and green glow. There were no signs of Romanescu.

"You think he's in here?" Murphy whispered.

"He's here," Hazeltine replied pointing at the floor. There was a spot of dark liquid; blood. Whether it was Romanescu's or his latest victim wasn't clear, but it was fresh.

We moved out into the middle of the dance floor. Between the security lighting and what light leaked in through the stained glass windows set high in the walls, we could make out shapes, but there were plenty of shadows. The pillars holding up the loft and balconies provided lots of hiding places. Murphy swung the beam of his flashlight around, but it didn't do much good.

"What's in the bottle?" I queried the professor.

"Holy water," he replied sheepishly. "Don't ask."

"Do you think it will do any good?"

"About as much good as you shotgun." Hazeltine had a point. I'd taken a couple of shots at the guy that so far hadn't slowed him down.

"Will you guys shut up. I don't think he's in this room. Maybe in there."

"There" was an adjoining room that held the pool tables. There was a wide opening off the far side of the dance floor leading into it.

The pool room was about thirty by forty feet long with a half dozen pool tables in two rows down the center. Some of the ubiquitous pews lined the sides and another bar ran along the front of the room.

It was darker in the pool room than it had been on the dance floor, the only light coming from a pair of exit signs and Murphy's flashlight. I nearly ran into the corner of one of the pool tables, and gave a low curse.

We could hear a faint sound, something between a whimper and a growl. It was coming from behind the bar.

"Come out, Romanescu," Murphy called. "We know you're there."

Suddenly Romanescu stood up. I pointed the shotgun at him, but the bar was shielding most of him. Murphy had him in the beam of his flashlight, his service revolver aimed at his head. The professor was doing what he saw as his part, holding the crucifix aloft while he tried to get the cap off of the vial of holy water with one hand.

"Do you think you can stop me?" Romanescu sneered. It would have been pathetic if he hadn't been so deadly.

"You're under arrest, Romanescu. Come out with your hands up." Part of me admired Murphy for playing it by the book; part of me was screaming "just shoot him."

We couldn't see Romanescu's hands because they were behind the bar. Suddenly he brought them up and threw a bottle of vodka at Murphy who had to dive to the side to avoid it. I let go with the shotgun, but he had ducked down behind the bar. I fired a second round into the bar, but I had my doubts as to whether the pellets would make their way through.

I looked around nervously, the shotgun still held at the ready. The professor had ducked behind one of the pool table. I couldn't blame him. I noticed that the bottle of holy water had dropped from his hand and rolled under the table.

We could hear noises behind the bar. Romanescu was moving, making his way along the bar. I debated letting off another blast, but I wasn't sure where he was. I'd let off three rounds already, and I'd left the extra shells back in the car.

All this time Murphy was making his way between the pool tables towards the bar. I could see what he was doing; he was heading towards one end of the bar where he'd have a clear shot all along the space behind it. I fired off another round to serve as a distraction. We were making a mess of the place, but I didn't care.

Murphy got into position and popped up, his pistol pointing along the bar.

"Damn," he cried. "He's not here."

"Where could he have gone?" I asked. It didn't take long to figure out. Behind the bar there was a narrow door leading to the cellar.

"Everybody OK?" Murphy asked.

"Yeah, I'm fine," I answered. "But I'm running low on shells."

"I'm fine," Hazeltine said. "I think we can rule out crosses and holy water as deterrents, though." He'd dropped the crucifix on one of the tables and picked up a pool cue, instead, holding it by the thin end like a baseball bat.

"OK. I'm going down after him. You guys don't have to follow, but I'll be damned if I'll let him get away this time."

35.

Of course we followed Murphy into the cellar.

It was about what you'd expect the cellar of a bar in a hundred year old building to look like. Cases of booze and beer were stacked up four or five high, there was a pile empty cartons waiting to be flattened and disposed of, kegs of beer waiting their turn in the cooler. The bar above may have been closed, but the stock hadn't been disposed of yet. On the way down the steep steps, Murphy had found a light switch, so at least we were no longer working in the dark.

Besides the steps we were on, the only other exit appeared to be a heavy metal door, presumably where they brought in deliveries. It had a couple of big padlocks on heavy duty looking hasps that gave the appearance of still being intact. If Romanescu had come down there, he was still there. Unfortunately, the basement offered plenty of hiding places.

"Guard the steps," Murphy ordered. "Don't let him get by you. I'll try to flush him out."

"Sure thing. And Murphy—"

"Yeah?"

"Be careful."

The detective just grunted and headed towards the loading door.

From my post at the foot of the steps I kept my eye on Murphy. I wasn't going to let Romanescu sneak up on him if I could help it. The professor was standing next to me trying to look in all directions at once. I could see the fear on his face. That hadn't stopped him from being there, though. You never know what a guy is like until you've seen him in a pinch. Hazeltine was holding up better than most.

I've said before how Romanescu seemed to be able to come out of nowhere. Well he did it again. He must have been hiding behind some boxes, but suddenly he was running down an aisle between two stacks, bearing down on me like a middle linebacker. I fired the shotgun, a blast that echoed in the confines of the cellar, but I must have aimed high. I worked the slide and pulled the trigger again, but all I heard was a click. I was out of shells. I tried to swap ends of the gun to use it as a club, but his shoulder plowed into me sending me sprawling.

When I looked up, Romanescu was standing over me, his eyes wild, his mouth still red from the blood of his last victim. I tried to find the shotgun, but it had slid across the floor when I fell.

That's when the professor hit him with the pool cue. It didn't do much to stop Romanescu, but it probably saved my life. Hazeltine had hit him square across the side of the head. He'd hit him hard, hard enough to shatter the cue so that the butt end went flying, a foot and a half long splinter of wood.

Romanescu spun on Hazeltine. I'd had to deal with a guy high on PCP once when I was a cop. He'd acted like he had super-human strength. It had taken four of us to get him under control; two had ended up in the hospital afterwards. Romanescu was like that. He picked the professor up and tossed him across the room. I heard a sickening crunch as something broke. Romanescu started towards him to finish him off.

I couldn't let that happen, not without trying to stop him. The only weapon that came to hand was the stub of the pool cue. The end where it had splintered was sharp and pointy. Not much of a weapon, but all I had.

I got to my feet clutching the cue like a knife. Calling out to him, I got Romanescu's attention away from the professor. He turned so that he faced me. There was a smile on his face. I think that's what did it.

I ran at him, going as fast as I could with one bad leg. I didn't know where Murphy was. I didn't care. It was going to end it then and there. I remembered what the professor had said. A stake to the heart. At that point I didn't know if Romanescu was a man or a vampire. I didn't care. All I knew was that a stake to the heart would kill him either way.

I must have looked as crazy as Romanescu. His eyes went wide. Then the point of the pool cue went into his chest. It went in up to where I was holding it in both hands. At the instant of impact there was an explosion. It was Murphy's service revolver going off. He had been a few feet behind me. I looked up and saw the hole appear in Romanescu's forehead where the .38 slug tore into his brain. I was still holding onto the end of the cue when his body slumped to the cement of the floor.

Murphy was standing there, his pistol ready to put another slug in Romanescu, but there wasn't any need. He was dead. After a moment, Murphy knelt down next to the corpse to feel for a pulse in his neck. He shook his head.

"You better check the professor," he said standing up again.

Hazeltine was just sitting up. A stack of boxes had broken his fall.

I asked him, "Are you OK?"

He nodded, then added, "My arm doesn't seem to be working right. I think I broke something."

"Don't move. We'll get someone to check you out."

"Yeah." His face had gone pale from the shock. "It hurts—" then "Is it over?"

"It's over. Murphy put a bullet through his brain. He's dead. For good measure, I put what was left of that pool cue through his heart."

"Don't take it out. Don't let them take it out, OK?" The professor sounded a little crazed, but I didn't blame him.

"Don't worry, professor," Murphy said. "No one is taking it out if I have anything to say about it."

A little while after that, a couple of uniforms showed up, then some more. One of them got on the radio and called for an ambulance for Hazeltine. It turned out he wasn't badly hurt, just a broken collar bone. I rode in the ambulance with him to the hospital. I figured that Murphy could handle things at the Church Pew.

They kept the professor in the hospital overnight. Me, I just found the nearest chair and fell asleep.

Of course, the newspaper made a big deal of the story. There was a timeline of the case and a list of the victims. Murphy was painted as a hero. I had no problem with that, the case had caused him a lot of sweat and tears. There had been a paragraph about the role played by Professor Hazeltine, both as suspect and as one who had been in on the kill. I was mentioned, too, briefly. At least they spelled my name right. After a day or so, some international crisis pushed the story off the front page.

It was never established just who Vladimir Romanescu was. It turned out his fingerprints didn't match those on file for the man that the State Department had granted asylum back in 1956. They never revealed what had happened to that Vladimir Romanescu, but by then, no one really cared.

Blood samples taken from Romanescu's body were found to contain half a dozen illegal drugs such as methamphetamine and PCP. That might well explain his seemingly superhuman strength and imperviousness to pain. That's the official theory, anyway.

36.

Romanescu was buried today. The professor had argued for cremation and the scattering of the ashes to the four winds, but a will turned up in some of the stuff he'd left behind at the House of Esoteric Wisdom. In it, Romanescu had specified what was to be done with his remains. His remains were to buried unembalmed in consecrated earth. He'd also bought a burial plot and prepaid for the internment. When the matter was brought to court, the judge was sympathetic with those who were opposed but decided that there were no legal grounds for him to disregard the wishes of the deceased. Hazeltine had argued that Romanescu should at least be decapitated and that the head should be placed face down in the coffin, but the Medical Examiner ignored that suggestion. With Romanescu dead, people who hadn't been intimately involved in the case were starting to think rationally again.

The M.E. didn't bother to conduct a full autopsy. Given the hole made by Murphy's .38 slug in the middle of Romanescu's forehead, it wasn't considered necessary. Somehow, the stub of the pool cue that I had driven through his heart never made it into the final post mortem report as they determined that that had happened after Murphy had taken his shot. It sounded better that way, and made the police look good. With the end of the case, some of the more embarrassing details were being glossed over for the public. I didn't particularly care; I wasn't looking for credit.

I'll say this for the M.E., though, they didn't remove the cue before they put the body in the coffin. I don't know if he was just playing it safe, or if he did it out of sympathy for the victim's families and those who had been part of the hunt.

There hadn't been any service, of course, just the men from the cemetery who would put the casket in the ground. No priest or minister said any words, either, as it was lowered down. There were a lot of people there, not as mourners but rather as witnesses, mostly family of the victims, but also various members of the press. There was a TV crew, too, but the footage never made it on the air as far as I know. And of course, Murphy, Hazeltine and myself. The professor's arm was still in a sling from the broken collar bone.

I'd called Vern Smerchek a few days earlier to tell him about the internment. He'd sounded drained as if he didn't really care about anything, anymore. He'd been polite, though.

"Thanks for letting me know," he'd said.

"It's the least I could do," I'd replied.

"I'm sorry for what I said, you know, before. I was just angry."

"You don't have to apologize, Mr. Smerchek. I understand. This has been a strain on all of us. It's taken its toll on everybody."

There was a long silence and I was about to say good-bye and hang up when Vern asked:

"It's really over now, isn't it?"

"Yeah. It's over. Romanescu is dead. They're sticking him in the ground in a couple of days."

"You were there, weren't you? At the end, I mean."

"Yeah, I was there."

"And he's really dead? You're sure?"

"Yes. He's really dead. Sergeant Murphy put a .38 bullet right between his eyes. You don't live after that." I know that now it sounds harsh, but at the time I figured that might be the only way that it would be real for Vern Smerchek.

"I heard that you drove a stake through his heart. Is that true?"

"Yes. It was the broken off stub of a pool cue not a stake, but I stuck it all the way in, eighteen inches of it."

"Is it still there?"

"Yeah. It's still there." The conversation was starting to depressing me. It was getting creepy, too. "It's over, Vern. I know you might not believe me, but you can start trying to rebuild your life. For Ellen and Katherine if not for yourself."

"Yeah. I guess you're right," he said, but I could tell he didn't believe me. "Thanks for calling. And thanks for all you've done."

There were no good-byes, just dead air.

Vern and Ellen Smerchek had been at the burial. He was wearing a brown suit and a tie, Ellen had on a black dress. What the hell do you wear to the burial of someone you hate, anyway, the burial of the man that killed your daughter and your dreams. I didn't talk to either of them.

The casket was lowered into the ground and the cemetery workers started covering it up using the backhoe they had used to dig the grave. Scoop by scoop the dirt covered up the coffin. One by one the onlookers started to leave. The TV crew packed up their equipment. In the end only Murphy, the professor and I remained.

Finally I said, "I could use a drink."

Epilogue Redux

They reinterred Romanescu's body today. This time there wasn't much of a crowd, just Murphy, Hazeltine, and myself. I guess that the others that had been at the exhumation were finally convinced that he was dead. The three of us were just there to make sure he went back into the ground without a hitch.

There wasn't much of a ceremony, just a couple of workers from the cemetery to take the coffin from the mortuary van. They hooked up the sling and lowered the casket into the hole that had laid empty since they'd dug him up. Afterwards, the back-hoe filled in the grave and tamped down the earth with the bucket. It all took less than fifteen minutes.

Dr. Morton, the M.E., had said that the authorities in Ohio had wanted tissue samples from Romanescu to match against samples taken from several crime scenes including the girl in the meat packing plant. It was something about DNA. He tried to explain, but it just went over my head. If it helps them close a couple of cases, it's fine by me, but what really matters is that Romanescu is back in the ground with a pool stick through his heart.

Some scientists with the university had taken the opportunity to take their own samples from the corpse. If they found anything unusual, they weren't saying. I guess I don't really care about that either, unless they find something that will prevent another Romanescu from happening.

After the workers were done with the grave Murphy suggested we go for a beer. He got no complaints.

We went to the same bar we'd gone to after the exhumation. It was quiet and convenient. Murphy sprang for a pitcher and we grabbed a table off in the corner where the bartender couldn't hear us. I guess we'd learned one lesson from the whole thing.

"Do you think it's finally over?" Hazeltine asked.

"It's never going to be over for Anna Smerchek's parents," I responded. "But, yeah, I think it's over as far as Romanescu is concerned. You can go back to teaching at the university."

"I'm not sure I can. Not after what I've seen," the professor said.

"What else are you going to do?" Murphy asked without much interest.

"Some people that I know out in Hollywood have asked me to write a treatment for a film about Romanescu."

"Great, that's all we need," Murphy said. "Another vampire movie. Are you going to do it?"

"I don't know. I really don't know."

We sipped our beer in silence after that. Finally Murphy spoke up.

"There's one thing I want to know."

"What's that?" I asked.

"Was there ever a time when—well, when you thought Romanescu might really be a vampire?"

"There are no such things as vampires, Sergeant," Hazeltine replied dryly.

"Sure. We all know that. But was there a point, Professor, where you knew that Romanescu wasn't human? After all, you know a lot more about that kind of thing than either of us."

"No. I can truly say that I was never sure that he was a vampire. But I can't say I was ever positive that he was not."

Murphy just grunted.

"There are lots of odd stories of things that have happened over the last few thousand years in remote corners of the world. I'm an English professor, not a scientist, but who's to say that some of them aren't true."

"I can't say if Romanescu was a vampire or not," I chimed in, "because I guess I really don't know what I mean. What I do know is that he was a monster. I've got no regrets at all about putting him in the ground. Only next time I'd use a bigger stake."

"I'll drink to that," the professor said, raising his glass.

"Do you think there will be a next time?" Murphy asked.

"I certain hope not."

For most people it's over. For some, though, like Anna Smerchek's parents, Luigi Bertoli and his brother, and some of the family and friends of the other victims it will never be over. And for Murphy, the professor and me, well I still wake up in a cold sweat after dreaming of Anna Smerchek's corpse laid out in that basement, the blood drained from her body. From things that Murphy has said, I know he does, too. I'm not sure about the professor, we haven't talked about it, but I have my suspicions. For us, it will never be over, either.

AUTHOR AFTERWORD

People sometimes ask where writers get their ideas from. In the case of *The Uncorrupted Corpse*, I can answer that with some exactness. The genesis for the novel came some four decades ago during a five hour nocturnal marathon where I wrote the first five thousand words of the novella *The Fictional Detective*. In that story a detective is hired to investigate the death of the mystery author Ezekial O. Handler. One of the books ascribed to Handler is *The Uncorrupted Corpse*.

At the time, I thought it was great title in search of a book, and in the intervening years I repeatedly tried to come up with a story line to wrap the title around. Thirty-five years after coming up with the title I began working on the book in ernest resulting in the current volume.

It certainly isn't the book that Ezekial Handler would have written. That book would have featured more sex if not necessarily more violence. Unlike my previous works, it is neither fantasy nor science fiction. In many ways it is very much a straight detective thriller though there are allusions to vampires and the supernatural.

For those readers interested in the more technical aspects of writing there are two points of note. One is that I never explicitly name the private detective narrating the story. There are precedents for this: Dashiell Hammett never put a name to his Continental Op in twenty some stories and two novels. It's not particularly easy writing dialog when one of your characters doesn't have a name, but once I started with the practice, I decided to persevere.

The second point of interest is that the book is divided into three sections of twelve chapters each. The events in each section center on the character after whom it is named. Somehow, this somewhat formal structure seemed appropriate for the subject matter.

I make no apologies for the fact that *The Uncorrupted Corpse* is a dark and bleak tale. That is the way the story wanted to unfold, and I let it have its way with me. It is also ambiguous in that there is no nice resolution at the end. I find lately that the ambiguous appeals to me. Despite these attributes, I hope that you, the reader, will find *The Uncorrupted Corpse* satisfactory.

Greg Fowlkes

SPECIAL PREVIEW!

A FICTIONAL DETECTIVE TRIFECTA

~ NOVELLAS FEATURING
THE FICTIONAL DETECTIVE ~

Now available from The Fictional Press
www.TheFictionalPress.com

A FICTIONAL DETECTIVE TRIFECTA:
THE FICTIONAL DETECTIVE
SPEAKS WITH THE DEAD

My name is Frank Slade. I'm a private detective. At least I think I am. Oh, I'm sure I'm a private dick, but some things about my last case have caused me to question my reality. I'm a man without a past. Before a few months ago there's nothing to prove I ever existed, no paper trail, no public record. My own memories from that time are all kind of vague and hazy. And generic, like they were details created by someone making them up. Like maybe someone named Ezekial O. Handler, the mystery writer that got bumped off not too long ago by his publisher. Oh, there are a few people who claim to have known me, like Flannigan, a police detective, but when I checked into it, his past is no more substantial than my own. Handler wrote me a letter in which he claimed he was responsible, that he had created me to avenge his death by means of some spell he had gotten out of an old book, just like he had created Flannigan, Armand the ex-jockey who operates a newsstand downstairs, a female impersonator named Josephine LaTouche, and Janet Nielsen, my fiancée and Handler's old girl friend. It was a pretty wild claim, even if it did seem to fit the evidence. But Handler had proved to have a good idea of the events that followed his death. If I were a thinking man, it might have bothered me, wondering whether I was real or not, but I'm just a simple private gumshoe and the whole thing is just too existential to worry about.

The current reality is that I'm a private detective with an office in a low rent building in a not particularly nice part of town. The office is what you'd expect would come out of the imagination of a mystery writer known more for his lurid titles than his high literary style. Of course, it's also just the sort of office a not terribly successful P.I. might rent. There's the frosted glass in the door with my name in peeling black paint, the second hand furniture, the bottle of bourbon stashed in the desk drawer.

It's the kind of office that you've seen at the start of a dozen mystery movies and read about in more pulp thrillers than you can count. I won't describe it in detail, you can visualize it perfectly without really trying.

Like I said, I'm a private dick, though my fiancée is trying to get me to quit. It's too dangerous she says, and after Handler left her the rights to his last book, the one published after he was killed, it's not like we're going to need the money. She says I should try my hand at writing, detective fiction stuff, says I'd be a natural at it, and wit the Handler connection I'd have no problem finding a publisher. What the heck. I might as well give it a try, so here goes. This is an account of my most recent case as it actually happened. It might even be real.

I was sitting in my office going through my files. This was a couple of weeks after I'd solved the Handler murder. That case had left me with a lot of unanswered questions about the nature of reality and I'd gone into a kind of funk that ended up in a week-long drunk. After I'd sobered up I came to the conclusion that no matter what the truth was, there was nothing I could do about it and I might as well just get on with life. After all, it wasn't shaping up as such a bad life. Janet and I were talking about getting married. Janet is the kind of dame men dream about; tall, good looking with curves in all the right places. She was smart and had money, too. We'd be fixed for life with what Handler had left her in his will.

I was thinking about getting out of the business, and was trying to tie up loose ends. I wasn't really looking for any new cases, but I was still listed in the phone book and business directory and it still said "Private Detective" under my name on the frosted glass in the office door. I wasn't completely surprised then, when there came a tentative knock on that door. It was a woman's knock, quick, light, not so much demanding attention as imploring for it.

I stood up, stashed the bottle of bourbon and the glass in the bottom drawer and went to open the door. The last time I had done that, the woman had been Janet, a leggy blonde with looks straight out of a fashion magazine. My visitor was nothing like that.

She was a big woman, not fat, but ample, probably in her mid fifties. She was dressed expensively in a dress and coat that actually fit her and made her seem thinner than she really was. Her hair had been styled recently in one of those cuts that women who can afford it wear. She reminded me as much as anything of the heavy set broad who always played the older rich dame in the Marx brothers movies. You know the one I mean, the one who never seemed to get the jokes.

"Mr. Slade?" she asked tentatively.

"That's me. What can I do for you?"

"I believe you are a—a private detective?"

"That's what it says on the door, though I'm thinking of getting out of the racket."

"Oh—I'm sorry. I thought—" I could see she had trouble on her mind. I never could turn down a dame in trouble, even an older one.

"Please, come in. The least I can do is hear your story. After all, you came all this way down here to talk to me."

"That's very kind, Mr. Slade." She entered the office and took the chair facing the desk. Despite her size she moved with a certain kind of grace. I shut the office door and sat in my desk chair.

When I was seated she said, "I don't quite know where to start."

"Why don't we start with the simple things. Like your name."

"Yes. Of course. I'm Geraldine DuVille. My husband was Herbert DuVille. He ran a trucking business, Tri-State Transportation Services, until he died recently."

"My condolences, Mrs. DuVille. Just what did you want to consult with me about?"

"Well, it's like this, Mr. Slade. Some time before his death, my husband took on some partners. He needed some capital to expand the business."

"How was the business doing, if you don't mind my asking?"

"Quite well, I think. I never bothered too much about the business. I left that to Herbert. But we had always lived quite comfortably. Herbert was a good provider." I could hear the love in her voice. "I'm not sure why Herbert felt the need to expand, but he seemed to think it was important."

"And these partners he brought on? Were they on the up and up?"

"They seemed to be at first. They were just going to invest some money and leave the running of the business to my husband. But after awhile they wanted to become more involved. He never said anything about it, but I could tell that Herbert wasn't altogether happy with the situation."

"Any particulars?"

"As I said, Mr. Slade, I never involved myself with the business. And then Herbert died, and that changed everything."

"Just how did he die?"

"An accident, or so I thought—"

"But something has caused you to change your mind?"

"I'm getting to that. The arrangement as I understand it was that my husband retained fifty-one percent of the company while Mr. McClure and Mr. Trentino split the remainder of the shares between them. However, there appears to have been an unfortunate clause placed in the contract by which they invested. In the event of the death of any of the partners, their share of the company would be split between the surviving partners. The result was that when my husband died his share of the company went to Mr. McClure and Mr. Trentino, and I was left with nothing."

"Your husband didn't leave anything to you?"

"Oh, no, Mr. Slade. I don't want you to think that. He left me the house, of course and some investments. There was also a large insurance policy that he had taken out shortly after we were married. I don't want you to think that he left me a pauper. I may not be able to live quite as well as before, but I shall get by. But it's the thought of the company that Herbert worked so hard to build just going to those— others that bothers me."

"You've talked to a lawyer about this, haven't you?"

"Yes. He said that it was an unusual agreement, but it seemed perfectly legal. He didn't hold out much hope for litigation, I'm afraid."

"I'm sorry about your troubles, Mrs. DuVille, but I'm not quite sure what it is you want me to do?"

"What I want you to do, Mr. Slade is come to a séance."

"A séance?" I said with surprise. It was about the last thing I had expected.

"Yes, a séance, Mr. Slade. I know that this may sound to you like a strange request, but I have been in touch with my husband, and he wishes to speak with you personally. There is something that he wants to tell you."

"You've talked to your husband? At a séance?"

"Yes."

"And he asked for me?" I couldn't keep the skepticism out of my voice.

"Yes. He was quite particular about that point. At the last session he asked for you. That's why I came down here, Mr. Slade. I assure you that I don't normally employ private detectives."

"I didn't think you did, Mrs. DuVille. I admit that I have very little experience with these kind of things, but isn't this an awfully specific request for someone who is dead to communicate."

"I assure you, Mr. Slade, that this séance was not a silly parlor game like those Ouija boards. The Professor is a very serious person."

"The professor?"

"Yes, the medium. Professor Longwell. He's quite well known, Mr. Slade."

"I'm sure he is." Probably by half the bunko squads in the state, I thought to myself.

"I detect a note of doubt, Mr. Slade, but I am willing to pay you for your time, whatever your standard rate is. Please, won't you come? I'm a desperate woman." She seemed on the point of tears.

"It's a hundred dollars a day. Plus expenses."

"What's a hundred dollars?"

"That's my standard fee, Mrs. DuVille. When is this séance?"

"Tonight, if you can make it. I'm sure I can arrange it with the Professor. He's been so helpful."

"I'm sure he has. As it is, I am available tonight. What time?"

"Would nine o'clock be possible?"

"That shouldn't be a problem." Janet was going to fix me dinner, but we'd be done in plenty of time.

"Fine. Here's the address," she handed me a card with her name and address.

"Tonight, then. And don't worry, you can pay me after the séance."

"Thank you, Mr. Slade. I'll be waiting for you."

She rose and I escorted her to the door.

After she left, I thought about the deal. Was she just some poor widow being preyed upon by a charlatan? Or was there more to this séance business? I didn't really believe in ghosts. On the other hand, I didn't not believe in them either. I'd seen enough strange things lately to keep an open mind. Of anyone in the world, I was the last to question the reality of such things. Or the reality of anything, for that matter.

I remembered reading about Herbert DuVille's death in the papers, but couldn't recall any of the details. It hadn't made much of a splash, just a few column inches in the financial section. The death had been ruled an accident. A jewelry heist the next day that had left two dead had pretty much seized my attention along with that of just about everyone else in town.

I decided to give my favorite flat-foot a call. He worked the homicide squad, and if there was anything about DuVille's death that hadn't made the papers, he'd be the one to know.

The phone rang three or four times before a voice announced, "Homicide, Lt. Flannigan." He didn't sound happy. Like he wasn't getting enough sleep.

"It's Frank. Got a minute?"

"Oh, sure, Frank. I've got plenty of time for cheap private dicks. After all, that's what we're here for, isn't it?"

"I can sense that you're busy, so I'll make it quick. What do you know about Herbert DuVille's death?"

"DuVille? It was ruled an accident. Some boxes fell on him at his warehouse or something like that. Why the interest?"

"His widow was just in my office. Apparently her husband has something he wants to tell me."

"Her husband, huh? Wait a minute. Is this some kind of gag, Slade? Her husband's dead."

"It's no gag, Flannigan. Or if it is, it's on me. She wants me to attend a séance. She claims her husband is going to communicate with me from beyond."

"Beyond what?"

"You got me."

"You're not taking this seriously, are you Frank?"

"I don't know. Like I said, his widow was in my office wanting to hire me. She seemed kind of upset. The way I figure, it's probably some huckster trying to take advantage of a poor widow that just happens to have some money. I thought I'd go to this séance and maybe find the hidden wires or whatever."

Flannigan said, "I thought you were thinking about getting out of the P.I. business, Frank."

"Yeah, I am. Janet doesn't like the idea of me putting myself in danger. But how much risk can there be at a séance?"

"I don't know, Frank. Some of these older dames can get some crazy ideas."

"I think I can protect myself. By the way, you wouldn't know anything about a Professor Longwell, would you?"

"Who's that?"

"He's the guy that's holding the séance. The medium."

"Not my line, Frank, but I can ask the guys in Bunko if they've ever heard of him."

"That would be swell, Flannigan. I'll be at Janet's until about 8:30."

"A hot dame like that, and you want to run around messing with ghosts. If you ask me, you're the crazy one, Frank."

"I get that a lot. Let me know if you find out anything. I'll let you get back to your corpses, Flannigan."

I found myself talking to a dead phone. Flannigan had cause for being short of patience. He had been putting in long hours working the jewelry heist murders. A salesclerk and the store's owner had been found dead. Over a million in prime ice was missing, too, without much in the way of clues.

I looked at the clock on the wall. It was getting late, and Janet was expecting me for dinner. I didn't want to disappoint her.

The Fictional Detective is available now from The Fictional Press. Find it on TheFictionalPress.com, or buy it on Amazon.com!

BOOKS BY GREG FOWLKES

From the Wizard at Law Series:
The Laws of Magic
Trial by Magic

From the Murder on Mars Series:
Blood Red Sands of Mars
A Death at Station Alpha
A Corpse in Hut Town
Murder at the Mars Club

From the Fictional Detective Series:
The Fictional Detective
A Fictional Detective Trifecta

Star City Stories: Space Opera Noir Featuring Frank Sladek

The Uncorrupted Corpse

Tequila Visions

Cargo From Paradise

Ice Viking

FROM THE WIZARD AT LAW SERIES BY GREG FOWLKES

THE LAWS OF MAGIC

Egil Njalsson was an aspiring lawyer. A lawyer with a difference. Not only had he passed the bar, but he had an undergraduate degree from the most prestigious school of magic in the country, the California Institute of Thaumaturgy. Needless to say his caseload and clients tended to the unusual. Like witches; or vampires. And the opposition, well they were likely to be demons. But Egil Njalsson had sworn an oath to uphold the law of the land, and... *The Laws of Magic*!

TRIAL BY MAGIC

Egil Njalsson is just another practicing attorney. Except, that is, for the occasional unusual client. Such as the ghost who retained his services using e-mail. Or the wolf who has been cursed by an Indian shaman to turn into a human during the full moon. Or the Leprechaun who is facing the loss of his saloon. Even when the clients are human, they have unusual problems like the Creole chef accused of making a rival a zombie or the scientist accused of transmuting a man into a statue of silicon. Yet somehow, Egil manages to resolve all his client's problems whether legal or magical. Of course it helps that he is a wizard as well as a lawyer.

Trial by Magic includes five new tales from the same world as *The Laws of Magic*.

FROM THE MURDER ON MARS SERIES BY GREG FOWLKES

BLOOD REDS SANDS OF MARS

On Mars the wind was rising. The grains of sand could be heard abrading the thin aluminum skin that was the only protection against the outside. On the far side of Olympus Mons a prospector lies dead in the sand. Inspector Erik McKernan, head of the handful of men that make up the small Martian police force must find the killer while threading the maze of corporate and international politics that govern the planet, and he must do it while trying to survive . . .*The Blood Red Sands of Mars!*

A DEATH AT STATION ALPHA

Station Alpha, a remote Martian research facility isolated by a planet wide dust storm. When one of the scientists is found murdered, it falls to Inspector McKernan to determine which of the remaining twelve people at the station wielded the fatal weapon. But, as the crime was committed in a locked laboratory with no possible access and all the suspects would seem to have unbreakable alibis, it will take all his skills as a detective to solve the puzzle of *A Death at Station Alpha*. Thirty years in the making, the long awaited sequel to *The Blood Red Sands of Mars*.

A Corpse in Hut Town

Hut Town is the remnants of the original Martian settlement; a collection of inflatable buildings abandoned by the Trust Authority and the mining corporations and now occupied by those catering to the baser needs of miners and construction workers in for a spree. But when a corpse is found in one of the service tunnels, Chief Inspector McKernan is called in.

He has plenty of questions. Who's body is it? How did they die? How did they get to Mars in the first place, and why weren't they missed? And the most important one on the Inspector's mind— are there any more bodies down there?

Murder at the Mars Club

The Mars Club was the sanctuary of the rich and powerful on Mars, so when one of the members is found dead, Chief Inspector is called in to solve the case as discretely as possible. Will the solution of the case prove to be the one man he'd least like to implicate?

FROM THE FICTIONAL DETECTIVE SERIES BY GREG FOWLKES

THE FICTIONAL DETECTIVE

Mystery writer Ezekial O. Handler has been killed in a suspicious car crash. Private detective Frank Slade has been hired by Handler's beautiful girlfriend to investigate. Handler, seemingly with a premonition of his death, has left a trail of clues. Can Slade discover the murderer, or will he instead uncover a secret that will shake his existence to the core?

A FICTIONAL DETECTIVE TRIFECTA

The Fictional Detective has gotten out of the Private Investigator game. Instead, he's trying to write hard-boiled masterpieces such as *Death Buys a Condo*. But despite the fact that the door of his office now says WRITER, some of his clients haven't gotten the word. And a strange lot of clients they are. A man that only contacts him during séances because, well, he's dead; a female impersonator who has inherited a house that's just a little too haunted for the market, and a small time gambler who's trying to end an affair with Lady Luck.

Three All New Novellas featuring the Fictional Detective!

The Fictional Press
www.TheFictionalPress.com

The Fictional Press is a small, independent press specializing in the publication of fictional works by emerging authors. If you are interested in bringing your fictional works to life in print as well as electronically, contact us! We can help!

Find out more at www.thefictionalpress.com.

www.ingramcontent.com/pod-product-compliance
Lightning Source LLC
Chambersburg PA
CBHW071258250626
47159CB00004B/1231